Taking Care

By

Cadee Brystal

Taking Care

By Cadee Brystal

ISBN-10: 0991441761
ISBN-13: 978-0-9914417-6-1

Dear Reader,

Welcome back to Miller's Bend! If you've been with me through the stories of Riley and Shelby, Andrew and Allison, and Matt and Ashley, I'm sure you're asking, "What about Tyler?"

Tyler's story may surprise you, but it's my favorite of the Lessons of Love in Miller's Bend series. It speaks to a deep and abiding love set in Tyler's heart long before the opening scene. It is a love so true that he would have locked it away and kept it as a silent secret, if things had gone the way they should have. But I don't want to say too much.

As always, I've tried to bring you compelling characters who live out stories that could be unfolding in the lives of people you know – because everyone has a story. The message, once again, is presented without the need for foul language, alcohol or overt sexual behavior.

Happy reading!
Cadee Brystal

THANK YOU

Thank you to the many readers who have become fans of the Miller's Bend books. I never guessed how popular the series would become!

I'm indebted to my parents, who taught my siblings and me the value of using language effectively. Thank you to my children who have contributed to the storylines, and to my husband who has become a technical advisor, as well as encouraging me to get the books published.

Special thanks to my volunteer collaborators, Jessica, Marlys, Terri, Jenny, Char and MaKayla. And to my husband for his ongoing love, support and advice.

Cadee Brystal

Miller's Bend Series

By Cadee Brystal

Wide Open Spaces

Breaking Free

Settling Down

Taking Care

"BE CAREFUL WHAT YOU WISH FOR."

Cadee Brystal worked for a weekly newspaper for years before she began to write the Miller's Bend books. At one point she wanted to purchase the newspaper business – after all, it is the American dream to own your own business. The idea didn't work out and Cadee was content to continue in her role.

She composed the Miller's Bend stories and was ready to begin the publishing process, when circumstances changed, and she suddenly owned a business. The long-forgotten dream was a reality! And the publishing of the books was put on hold.

Cadee learned that plans and dreams can change or multiple plans can mesh into a new dream, even more fulfilling than its predecessor.

Similarly, the characters of Tyler and Chrissi learn that they can adapt to circumstances and move forward to new and potentially better dreams.

Cadee hopes you enjoy *Taking Care*, a contemporary Christian novel which encompasses messages of Christian faith applicable in our contemporary lives.

CONTENTS

CHAPTER ONE

Darkness wrapped around the two-door coupe, pushing against the driver's side window. Illumination from the car's headlights sliced into the abyss only to be swallowed up by the ever-thickening fog. Visibility had diminished to a few yards and Chrissi Gibson pulled the car carefully nearer to the edge of the highway where she continued to creep along at less than ten miles per hour. The driving conditions forced her to focus on what was right in front of her ... instead of the greater goal of reaching Miller's Bend, South Dakota. *Just move forward a few feet at a time and you'll get there,* she thought to herself.

A few short months ago, the world had been wide open. Filled with options and opportunities, her future had danced before Chrissi in a teasing and tantalizing way. Even though Chrissi was still a senior in Miller's Bend High School, she'd had her eighteenth birthday, and felt a surge of independence. She had received acceptance letters from three universities and had garnered several scholarships.

The previous two summers, she had worked in the hospital in Sioux Falls while staying with friends of the family. Chrissi had amassed hundreds of hours in the neonatal ward, and with each hour, her determination to become a neonatal nurse had grown. She found that she loved the work and possessed a natural affinity for connecting with the mothers as well as caring for the tiny infants whose needs were so great.

And now? Now Chrissi's life had changed. Her focus on the long-term goal of building the career she yearned for would need to shift. It had already begun to shift at the first hint that something was wrong. No, not wrong; just different. Today's appointment confirmed her suspicions. During the two-hour drive back home, Chrissi struggled to face the fact that everything would be different from today forward. Instead of looking down the road – to college and internships – Chrissi would be forced to accept and move on with the daily challenges she would be facing.

Chrissi glanced to the rear view mirror in an automatic response to the sudden flash of headlights behind her. With the heavy cloak of darkness on this late winter night, compounded by the thick fog, she hadn't noticed the approaching vehicle until it was practically on top of her own. Even though later she would tell herself that it was the worst thing she could have done, Chrissi reacted by braking and jerking the steering wheel to the right.

The sporty little red car spun wildly out of control ahead of him in the highway and Tyler Schuster silently cursed himself. He'd been driving like an idiot, trying to get back to Miller's Bend in the miserable weather. With his mind leaping from business concerns to his family, he had picked up speed without realizing it. The roads were treacherous; visibility was extremely limited. He had no business speeding along as if he were the only person out tonight.

The driver of the other car had apparently been being careful enough, but when Tyler and his big 4x4 Chevy truck popped over a little rise, he must have startled the other driver. He'd seen the brake lights flash before the rear end of the car had whipped to the left, passing the front end of the Grand Prix, as it spun into the ditch. The roads were too slick for a quick stop, but Tyler managed to avoid a collision.

With a quick prayer for the other driver's safety, and that no other vehicles would come rocketing over the crest of the hill, Tyler carefully stopped his truck. Putting it into reverse and watching for more traffic, he backed up in the traffic lane. His father, the town's police chief for many years, would kill him for such recklessness if he ever found out. At the thought of his father, Tyler's temper flared. Not his father – just the man who had raised him. Raised him and lied to him for all those years. And with that, the anger was back, burning through Tyler once again.

He parked on an approach at an angle that allowed the light cast from his headlights to reach the car in the ditch. Tyler threw the door open and stepped out, sinking into the winter's accumulation of snow, which had been decaying in the sunshine of recent days. Not feeling the scrape of the icy crust as he broke through with each step, Tyler progressed quickly to the driver's side of the car.

As a trained first responder, Tyler quickly assessed the situation: the car was stationary and in a stable location. It wasn't positioned to shift, fall or sink – thank goodness. And it hadn't actually collided with anything – it had spun out of control and come to rest deep in the snow-filled ditch. The driver probably had not suffered any serious injuries. Probably.

Dirty ditch snow filled the grill and packed the headlights, diminishing the illumination from them. Tyler registered the purr of the motor as he drew nearer to the vehicle and rushed to the driver's side door. Yanking it open, he spoke quickly, "Turn it off. Turn off the engine!" And then, without waiting for the driver to comply, he reached in front of the woman, felt along the steering column and then across the dash until his fingers brushed the key. He quickly turned it to kill the engine and jerked the key ring from the ignition.

"Are you hurt?" Tyler queried before turning to look fully at the driver who kept her head bowed. Her dark hair fell like a curtain to hide the woman's identity. He glanced at her hands, which bore no jewelry. "Who are you? What is your name?" he asked too quickly to allow her to answer. Then the driver raised her head, leaned back against the seat and turned her bright blue eyes, brimming with tears, on him.

Tyler's throat tightened and his chest restricted. *Chrissi!* His careless driving had forced Chrissi off the road. What if she'd have been hurt? He pushed his personal reaction aside and asked again, "What's your name?"

"I'm Christina Kay Gibson," she said clearly. "Tyler, you know full well what my name is." Then with a nearly unnoticeable quaver in her voice, she added, "Can you pull me out?"

His mind registered that she'd answered correctly, with no slurring or other warning signs, but he continued with the first responder evaluation, rather than answer her question. "Where are you? What time of day is it?" he demanded. Tyler's hands were sliding along Chrissi's scalp feeling for bumps, knobs or bruises, as he knelt on the doorframe.

She pushed his hands away. "Ty! I'm not a patient," she scolded. "I'm your friend. Now help me get back on the road. Please." Chrissi's plea was accentuated by the fearful hint in her expression, as their gazes caught and held. "Please," she whispered.

"I can't pull the car out – not without a winch and some help," he replied. "But I'll get you back home safely." She released the seat belt and began to turn in the seat, but Tyler's firm grip on her shoulders stayed her movement. "Answer my questions first. Where are you?"

"South of Miller's Bend on the state highway," she replied, her voice crisp with impatience. "I'd say about six miles from town."

The pressure in Tyler's chest eased. *This* was the Chrissi he knew and ... "What time is it?" he pressed.

"Suppertime, Ty," she said with a laugh. "And I'm tired and hungry. Can we go to town, please?"

His riveting silvery grey eyes twinkled as the light reflected, and a smile lit his features. "Sure," he cajoled. "Just tell me where you're hurt."

"I'm not hurt," came the assertion from the accident victim. "Just shook up."

Satisfied that she was fine, Tyler straightened and stepped back, allowing Chrissi room to step out of the stranded car. "I'll get the guys to help me get the car out tomorrow, so don't leave anything that you need," he informed her as the door slammed closed. He pulled the keys from his coat pocket and hit the lock button.

The weather conditions were not the deadly cold that existed a few weeks earlier in heart of the winter, but the air was sharp with moisture and a breeze whipped at their coats. "Let's get you home. You have everything you need?" he asked, gesturing toward the bag she'd shouldered and the shopping bag she clutched to her chest.

"I have what's important," she said quietly as she took the first step toward the waiting pickup. He snatched the parcels from Chrissi, thinking he could at least lighten her load. They didn't speak as they trudged through the snow. Tyler pressed ahead to open the trail, hoping to make it easier for Chrissi to make the trek. He was short, only about five and a half feet tall, but his work as a landscaper kept his muscles toned and his body strong. Tyler had no problem pushing through the snow, and was soon outdistancing Chrissi. He turned and watched her progress as he waited for Chrissi to catch up. She was about the same height, but with a slight build. And, Tyler reminded himself, that at least physically, she'd seemed almost fragile in the weeks since returning from her ordeal in Chicago.

"You're almost here, Chris," he offered in encouragement. "Just make it to me and you'll be fine."

Chrissi's steps faltered at hearing the words Ty spoke. She understood the context in which he'd spoken them – simple encouragement to help her make it to the safety and comfort of the pickup, which stood idling a dozen yards away. But her heart translated the phrase to a deeper, more profound declaration. If only that statement could be applied to her life; if only it was as simple as reaching Ty, and everything would be fine.

He must have seen the vulnerability in her eyes, because before Chrissi even had a chance to react, her friend was beside her, handing the packages back to her. A shiver racked her body as she asked, "What … what are you doing?"

"Let me help you," he replied in a rough voice. "I'll carry you …" He was ready to sweep her up into his arms, but she was relieved that Ty didn't make a move to touch her until she nodded. She curled into his embrace and closed her eyes as he took the first few steps.

Chrissi was tempted to let her mind accept the comforting thought that Ty might actually care about her as a person, as a woman. But in reality, she reminded herself, he only saw her as the annoying little sister of his best friend. It would be best to remember that – she was nothing to him beyond a sisterly pest. And now he was trudging through the crusted, dirty snow to get her to safety. No. Definitely no romantic notions involved there.

By the time the pair reached the pickup, Tyler was fuming. He wasn't upset with her. He was angry at himself for not paying more attention before, for not realizing the condition that Chrissi had let herself slip into. Even wrapped in her winter coat, she couldn't weigh a hundred pounds. He didn't offer to set her on her feet, but directed the woman in his arms to open the passenger door. Warm, inviting air rushed out of the cab as he nestled her onto the seat. He wanted to scold her for letting herself lose so much weight, but was afraid such words would damage their friendship. So he bit back the comment and let out a sigh as his gaze slid over her form, and just before he closed the door, he spotted her footwear. He didn't know what that style of shoe was called, but he knew her feet had to be nearly frozen.

Chrissi watched with growing discomfort as Tyler rounded the front of the pickup. Something had upset him and she thought she'd heard an oath as he'd slammed the door beside her. The suspicion was confirmed when he jerked open the driver's side door and reached into the back seat of the extended cab truck as he continued muttering. He pulled a blanket from the seat and handed it to her before jumping into his regular spot and closing the door. He pulled off his gloves, laying them on the dash. Tyler pushed the heater blower to high and bent down to grab Chrissi's feet, twisting her in the passenger seat to face him. Without comment, he flipped her flimsy shoes off and clasped her frigid feet between his warm hands.

At first, she only registered the pressure of his hands, but has Ty alternately held her feet and rubbed them, she felt the warmth begin to seep into her skin. "They're better now," Chrissi offered as pulled one foot away and began to rub it herself. "Thank you."

A sigh passed Tyler's lips before he slowly released her other foot. "Where are your winter boots? You could have gotten frost bite," he said quietly. "What if I hadn't come along?"

In the dim glow cast by the dash lights, he saw the indignation in her expression and the eyebrows rise in challenge before she retorted. "If you hadn't come along, I wouldn't have spun off the road into the ditch. I'd be home having my supper."

It was a valid point. If it hadn't been for Tyler and his sudden appearance behind her car, she may have made it safely home. That didn't matter to him though, as the frustrations and concern for her bubbled to the surface. "And what would that supper have been? An apple? Peanut butter toast?" he asked, barely disguising the accusation. "Why haven't you been taking care of yourself, Chris?"

Tyler watched as her brows drew down over her pretty blue eyes – there was an instant spark in their depths, but it quickly faded. She'd opened her mouth as if to refute the statement, but mutely closed it again. She let her focus drift down to the packages that had slid to the floor and shrugged. When she didn't respond, Tyler reached over and lightly pushed her hair back along her cheek. He thought she winced away a fraction of an inch, but she didn't look at him.

"Chris?" he whispered. Still she did not answer; she did not raise her gaze to his. Tyler had known Chrissi for most of her life because she was the sister of his best friend, Matt Vander Meer. If she'd decided not to talk, there wasn't a thing on Earth he could do to change her mind. And, he thought with mild amusement, when she did decide to talk, he'd have just as much trouble making her stop. Instead of pushing the issue – whatever it was – he opted to offer support. "If you need help, or decide you want to talk about it, you can count on me. Okay?" he said softly as he pulled his hand back. "Okay, Chris?"

She still didn't answer, but did meet Tyler's gaze for a moment before she nodded in silent agreement. The sadness and confusion he saw in her eyes nearly pushed Tyler to ask again, but he stopped himself. "Buckle up and I'll get you to town," he ordered. "You can close your eyes and rest … it'll take a while to get there with this visibility."

Cadee Brystal

CHAPTER TWO

Chrissi had been through a lot in the past couple of months. Tyler reflected that she had left Miller's Bend after Christmas on a mission to help her cousin, Maddy, who lived in Chicago. Being a headstrong, independent, intelligent woman, Chrissi had not been swayed when Matt told her she shouldn't go. Of course, Matt was her big brother and thought it was his responsibility to protect her, even though she was over 18 and legally an adult. Chrissi had secretly gone to Colorado where she met her father, Byron Gibson, and got additional money and a new cell phone for the rest of her trip. Meanwhile, Matt engaged the local law enforcement officials who used their resources to try to find Chrissi. They'd caught up with Byron, who told them she was headed to Chicago.

Tyler had been in the information loop throughout all of this because of his friendships with Matt, and Mason Alexander, who served as the family's lawyer. Tyler also acknowledged that his own father, or the man who he had *believed* to be his father, had fed him information as well because, as the local police chief, Jeff Schuster had access to it. And as Tyler's father, Jeff had known that Tyler cared about Chrissi, and had wanted to help ease his concerns.

The pickup reached the edge of town and the city streetlights battled the darkness, drastically improving the visibility. Tyler shifted his attention to the woman in the seat beside him. She had closed her eyes as he suggested and was likely asleep now. What had she gone through while she'd been away from Miller's Bend? What had happened? And why was she losing so much weight? She shifted her position, possibly in response to the light from the street lamps.

Tyler considered taking Chrissi to her mother's place, or even Matt's place. He figured she'd intended to be taken to her own apartment in the basement of Mrs. Holmes' house, and she might be mad, but he decided to take her to his father's place for supper. There would be plenty of nutritious, tasty, home-cooked food since Tyler and his father, Jeff, had been working on eating their way through dozens of casseroles that the townspeople had delivered when Jeff was hospitalized following the shooting.

The shooting. Tyler winced as he was reminded of the great and horrible day – the day that Chrissi returned to Miller's Bend. Two men died and Jeff Schuster was shot in the line of duty. It was the day Tyler learned that Jeff Schuster was not his father.

Chrissi had been present for the shooting. In fact, they'd determined later, she'd been the target when the gunman burst into the interrogation room at the police station and started shooting. She'd been through a lot, alright. And, Tyler realized, he didn't have a clue what had happened to Chrissi while she was in Chicago. He also realized that whatever had happened to her would impact Chrissi's life forever.

Tyler parked in the driveway of the house where he'd grown up. Jeff had been aware for weeks that something was wrong between the two of them, but Tyler had staunchly refused to talk about it – to reveal that he had learned the lie. Jeff wasn't his father.

Curling his fingers tightly around the steering wheel, Tyler glanced again at the woman beside him. "You're going to be okay, Chris," he said softly as she stirred. Her eyelids fluttered and opened, and then she smiled up at him. "Still hungry?" he asked.

She nodded and glanced out the window, and seeing Tyler's childhood home, she froze. "Why are we here?"

"I thought you could join me and … Dad for supper," he answered. "We have loads of food people have brought by since he was released from the hospital. Maybe I'll even send a casserole home with you."

She nodded in response. By the time Tyler had rounded the front of the pickup and opened the passenger door, she had her shoes on and had pushed the blanket away. He offered her a hand as she slid out of the vehicle, and hovered near as they walked to the side door of the house. Tyler helped Chrissi out of her coat, and hung it and his own on the chair near the exit. Before he took another step, Jeff called out from the living room, "Tyler? That you, son?"

"Yeah. It's me," he replied with little enthusiasm. He directed Chrissi to a chair by the table and proceeded to pull a container from the refrigerator and start it heating in the microwave. When Tyler turned from the task, he found Jeff leaning against the doorframe between the two rooms, silently glancing between Chrissi and himself.

"Evening, Chrissi," the older man said at length. "How ya been?"

"Fine. Thank you," Chris answered politely. "Yourself?"

13

"I've seen better days," Jeff replied as he slowly maneuvered into one of the chairs at the table. "Recovery takes a lot out of a person."

Their guest responded with a nod and added knowingly, "It surely does." Other than the hum of the microwave, the room was silent.

Tyler watched Jeff, who was recovering from the gunshot wound to his shoulder. They'd been lucky that he hadn't been killed. At the age of 56, Jeff had served the community as the police chief for decades, and had never even been forced to draw his weapon until the day of the shooting. He'd managed people with kindness and authority over the years. He had even begun to talk about retiring and "letting one of the young pups take over responsibility for the town". Tyler thought it was foolishness, but looking at the man who had loved him and raised him, Tyler could now see the signs of wear and tear. Jeff was tired – exhausted. Over the years he'd lost a good amount of hair and gained a good amount of girth. And in the aftermath of the shooting, just getting from one room of the house to the other was a major undertaking. He wasn't the vibrant, charismatic community leader he had once been.

But he was trying, Tyler acknowledged. Jeff was striving to recover from the wound that could have ended his life. And Tyler's self-centered behavior had been a roadblock to that goal.

His focus shifted to the young woman seated beside Jeff. She, too, was a fighter – striving to recover from her psychological wounds. The outer world couldn't see the effects of her ordeal, but to Tyler, they had become clear. She wasn't the bubbly, optimistic, confident young woman he had admired for the past couple of years. She was more quiet and reserved.

And Tyler knew in his heart that he wanted to help her through the dark times; he wanted to help her get back to the person she'd been before.

The microwave dinged, and as Tyler pulled the dish from its interior, he silently asked the Lord how he could help these two people for whom he cared so much, in their recoveries. He placed the bowl on a hot pad in the center of the table and retrieved the place settings from the cupboard, and milk from the refrigerator.

Before they dug in, Jeff offered a brief prayer, asking that the Lord to bless the food, thanking Him for the generosity of the townspeople, and asking that He continue to provide a healing touch in all their lives.

Unfortunately, in order to begin the healing process, a person sometimes must irritate the wound to get to the heart of the problem. "So Dad," Tyler began slowly, "I've been doing some reading."

"That's good. A man should never stop learning," Jeff replied as he took a bite of the casserole. When Tyler didn't elaborate, he asked, "What are you studying now? Some new plant varieties for the nursery?"

Chrissi glanced up from her meal, waiting to hear about the greenhouse. Tyler had started up his own business five years earlier, when he was only 22 years old. In the early years of the nursery, Chrissi had enjoyed hanging around while her brother, Matt, would lend a hand from time to time. She had even worked at the landscaping and nursery center as her summer job one year.

She noted that Ty didn't look happy and excited as he usually did when he discussed his business. He looked … apprehensive. "Maybe it should wait," Ty replied in a deflated tone. Nervously he glanced away from Jeff and his gazed skimmed the perimeter of the room.

Jeff laid his fork on the edge of his plate and clasped his hands. "I'm ready to listen anytime you need me," he replied.

The words and the voice of the man who had lovingly raised Tyler drew his attention and he looked again into Jeff's face. Tyler reached out to gently touch Chrissi's hand before he apologized, saying, "I'm sorry that you had to be here for this. I didn't plan it this way."

She didn't pull her hand away and her gaze caught Ty's. She didn't know what the ensuing conversation would be about, but could see – had seen for weeks – that he was distressed over something to do with his father. She didn't feel it was appropriate for her to be here, to witness the conversation. "I can go … I'll just call Mom and see if she or Matt can pick me up," she offered.

Ty shook his head in denial of the idea. "I'd like to see you home, and I'd rather not have your family wondering what's going on in our family. Besides … it might be good to have an innocent bystander here. A witness, if you will," he replied. And then he added, "I want you here."

When Tyler swung his attention back to his father, Chrissi busied herself clearing the table. Both men had pushed their plates away and it was clear that the fellowship of the meal had ended. She reflected on the way the friendship between Ty and herself had grown since the day she'd returned to Miller's Bend – each of them seemed not only to see, but to identify with the pain the other felt. They had connected when no one else in either family had noticed the struggles they were going through. As they began spending more and more time together, even though neither revealed the source of their distress, both found comfort in the relationship.

Chrissi mentally shook herself. She and Ty didn't have a relationship. And because of their nine-year age difference, and other reasons, they never would. Just friendship. Theirs was a friendship that had begun with Chrissi being the little sister who tagged along with her older brother. Matt and Ty and Riley Wheeler had been the best of friends for as long as Chrissi could remember. They were so close that at times it had been almost as if she had three brothers instead of one.

Although Chrissi willed herself not to overhear, it was impossible. Jeff began speaking and she could hear in the quality of his voice that he was concerned for his son. "What's the matter, son? I've known something's been eating away at you for weeks now. I figured you'd come to me when you were ready," he said.

As Tyler studied Jeff in recent weeks, he had realized how much the man loved him. They'd been through almost three decades together and Tyler had never once questioned the depth of emotion they shared. Tyler wondered whether raising the question of his paternity would destroy their relationship. If he didn't ask, would the lingering distrust damage it more?

Tyler squirmed. Did he really want the answer badly enough to lose the only family member he had? And then it was clear to him. No. He would bury his suspicions and move forward.

Something must have shown in his expression because, in the moment while Tyler searched for the words to back away from the topic, Jeff stiffened in his chair. His skin paled, his features tightened and he drew a shaky breath. "Oh, Lordy," he whispered roughly. "You found out didn't you?"

The air in the room pulsed before Tyler found his voice. "No. I've found out nothing," he answered. Chrissi could hear the restraint in Ty's voice; she could see the disillusionment in his eyes. "I only have questions," he said with an icy calmness.

"We … you're mother and I … we adopted you when you were a tiny infant," Jeff said slowly. "Circumstances put you in our care and we adopted you."

Chrissi froze at hearing the words. This was the issue that had Tyler turning away from his father? A secret, kept for 27 years, had been exposed. "Oh, Ty." The words slipped past her lips as she stepped to his side and laid a hand on his shoulder. Tyler seemed to lean into her touch.

"Adopted," he echoed. He reached up and placed his rough hand over Chrissi's in acknowledgment of her support, but didn't look at her. Keeping his gaze on Jeff, Tyler asked, "But why not tell me? Why keep it a secret? Why did you choose to lie to me?"

"It wasn't a lie -"

"It wasn't the truth!" Ty countered. "The truth is you are not my father," he added with quiet desperation. He lowered his face, hiding behind his hands.

Jeff's confident words worked their way into Tyler's heart. "I am your father and I have been since the moment I first held you in my arms. Fatherhood has far less to do with biology than it has to do with love. I am your father. I always have been and I always will be."

Mutely, Chrissi slid into a chair and waited. She could see that Jeff's words had been the ones Ty needed to hear, but there was more he needed. She silently willed the two men to listen to each other, not only with their ears, but also with their hearts.

Tears glistened in their eyes, but neither spoke for several minutes as they worked through their feelings.

"Why? Why didn't you tell me?" Tyler pleaded in frustration. "Why did I have to get my first clue when I was in the hospital, praying that you would survive? Why hadn't you told me?"

Chrissi's emotional connection to Ty, and the empathy she felt for both men, had tears trickling down her cheeks as she waited. She wanted to offer comfort but didn't know how. Unexpectedly, Ty reached across the table and clasped her hand. He held on to her as if he would drown if he let go. But his gaze remained on Jeff.

"I'm sorry, son. I should have told you years ago," Jeff conceded. "It was a mistake not to trust you with the truth. But you know that I love you, and that your mother loved you. That's what's important."

"It is," Ty replied. "But trust is important, too."

Jeff's color had improved, and Chrissi was glad to see it. "Maybe I should make coffee," she offered by way of shifting the conversation. Neither man acknowledged her statement, but Tyler's grip on her hand tightened as if to say, "No, stay with me."

Jeff's eyes narrowed as he watched his son. "What happened at the hospital?" he asked. "What made you suspect?"

"You'd lost a lot of blood from the gunshot wound," Tyler began to explain in a detached way. "I was at the hospital and you were in surgery. There was nothing I could do but pray. And after begging for you to survive so many times, I kind of thought ... I had to find something beneficial to do. I figured the hospital was using a lot of blood from their supply, with both you and the shooter they had in emergency surgery. So I went to the nurses' station and told someone that I wanted to give blood to help replenish the stock."

He continued, "She went to check with someone else, and that nurse came and told me they didn't have the man-power to spare to do that at the moment. Besides, she said they'd pulled my record and my blood couldn't be given to either of the emergency patients anyhow because of our blood types."

Releasing Chrissi's hand, Tyler surged to his feet and leaned toward his father. "Blood, Dad," he said coldly. "We don't match."

Chrissi's basic knowledge of medicine kicked in and she spoke up. "That doesn't mean you aren't father and son," she contributed. She'd learned about this in a pre-college course she'd taken in the fall semester. "Each parent contributes one allele toward the offspring's blood type. Your mother's blood type would have an effect."

Jeff frowned. "But I'm O. That's universal, right?"

"Universal donor," Chrissi confirmed. "But not as a recipient. With an O blood type, you can only receive type O blood." She looked to Tyler. "I take it you are not type O?"

"No. I'm type A," he answered darkly. His expression softened marginally as he focused on Chrissi for the moment. "I knew that what I'd learned at the hospital wasn't conclusive. I went online and did a quick search … I learned that a type O parent can have a type A child if the other parent was either A or AB."

Chrissi explained, "AB is very rare … I think the occurrence is only around four percent of the Caucasian population."

"That matches the information I found," Tyler confirmed, before returning his attention to Jeff. "You made it through surgery and into recovery. Dr. Stapp came and told me you were stable, but I wouldn't be able to see you for more than a couple minutes. So I did. I saw you and held your hand and then I remembered that as I had knelt next to you in the interrogation room after the shooting, before the ambulance arrived, you'd whispered that you loved me … and that you were sorry. And that's when I started to wonder just what it was that you were sorry for."

"Tyler. Son, I was sorry for being shot," Jeff croaked with dammed up emotion. "I thought I was dead. I was sorry for leaving you alone. For the things I would miss …" He glanced quickly at Chrissi and away just as fast before he continued quietly, "your wedding, my grandchildren. I was sorry for you … for the milestones in your life that you would have to face without a parent. But also for myself - because I would miss those milestones, too."

"You didn't mean you were sorry for lying to me?" Tyler challenged.

The older man refuted the statement, "No Tyler. I was thinking of the future; I wasn't thinking of the past."

"So you're not sorry for the deception?"

"Yes, I am," Jeff asserted. "But I can't change it. We can learn from it; but we can't change it."

"Maybe. At any rate, I left your bedside when the nurses made me. I went home, but it was lonesome," Tyler confided. He'd gone to the apartment he had shared with Matt for a couple of years, but Matt had been living with his and Chrissi's mother while she had undergone cancer treatments. The space had been empty and cold as he obsessed over Jeff's health and mortality. Tyler had fled from the apartment, just as he had fled from the hospital. He couldn't think of any place to go other than his childhood home – where he had always found comfort. But he discovered that it wasn't the home, but his father, who had supplied the comfort.

Tyler told his father, with Chrissi looking on, how after he'd rattled around in the house for hours before he'd driven aimlessly only to wind up back at Jeff's home that night - the night following the shooting. It was there, while he cried and prayed and mourned, that Tyler had remembered the hidden box of his mother's belongings. Jeff had stashed away a few treasured remembrances of his wife after her death. Tyler unearthed it and began going through the items: her wedding band, and some other jewelry, some cards from Jeff, photos of her – smiling and crying - holding Tyler as a baby, her diploma, her elementary school enrollment form which had included her parents' names, her birthplace and birthdate, eye color, hair color and blood type. And that was when he'd found the evidence – his mother's blood type had been O – that led Tyler to the conclusion that Jeff wasn't his father. He hadn't made the jump that his mother hadn't been his biological mother either, until the moment Jeff had declared, "We adopted you."

Raggedly, Tyler asked, "Who knows about this? How many people have looked at me over the years and said to themselves, 'Oh, that poor boy – he doesn't even know he's adopted.' Who knows the truth?"

"It's not like that. There was only your mother and I, one member of the birth family and an old lawyer who passed away shortly after the agreement was finalized," Jeff explained.

No one spoke for several minutes, and then Tyler rose from his chair. He slipped into his coat and helped Chrissi into hers. As he turned the knob to open the door, Jeff asked quietly, "You'll be back tonight?" Tyler looked back, nodded almost imperceptibly and followed Chrissi through the door, closing it tightly behind him.

CHAPTER THREE

Tyler's muscles burned and his breath stood heavy in the thick morning air as he scooped shovelful after shovelful of decaying snow away from the front of the Grand Prix - Chrissi's car that was stuck deep in the ditch a few miles south of town. A thick crust of snow mixed with wind-driven dirt formed the crusty top layer, but the layer below had turned mealy. After breaking the crust, it was like trying to shovel Styrofoam beads. It would be horrible stuff to attempt to gain any traction in. The trio of men would need to winch the car up to the approach and then pull it with a shorter chain onto the roadway.

Having arrived before Matt and Riley, Tyler cleared the snow away from the tailpipe of the car and started the engine. He'd taken the scoop shovel and dug the snow away from in front of all the tires, and pulled the snow from beneath the car's chassis. When he had completed those tasks and the other two men hadn't shown up, Tyler began shoveling a path toward the approach.

Tyler didn't stop to check the time. He just kept digging: *break the crust, scoop the snow and don't think about what you found in the car. Break the crust, scoop the snow and don't think about Chrissi. Break the crust. Scoop the snow.*

25

"Hey!" a familiar voice called from somewhere to Tyler's left, near the approach.

Don't think.

"Tyler!"

"What?!" he hollered in reply. Straightening to look toward Matt and Riley who had finally arrived, Tyler realized that he must look like a man possessed shoveling snow such a distance from the stranded vehicle.

His anger and frustration from the previous night's confrontation with his father had simmered for hours, relieved only by the brief time he'd spent when he picked Chrissi up from her apartment this morning to give her a ride to school. Chrissi and the growing relationship between the two of them were blessings in his life, and Tyler had finally admitted to himself that what he felt for her was real. He'd been so thankful that she'd been there when he first talked with his father about his paternity; that she'd been supportive and …

"What did you call us for, buddy?" Riley asked with a laugh as the two men trudged through the snow, following the path Tyler had taken. "Looks like you plan to dig it out all by yourself."

It was a good-natured barb, but by the time his friends had arrived he was feeling anything but good natured. "What took you so long? Did you stop for eggs and bacon at the Hot Spot?" Tyler countered, referring to the local truck stop at the junction of two major highways.

Matt grinned and his blue eyes sparkled with happiness. He replied, "Nope. Haven't had a bite to eat yet this morning. Let's get this show on the road and we can all go get breakfast together."

Matt's contented joy was usually pleasant, but today it was just another irritant to Tyler. "Well, I think I've done enough shoveling," Tyler commented as he passed the tool Matt. "Have at it. I'll run the winch."

Riley's hand pressed against Tyler's chest as he stopped Tyler's retreat toward the truck that sat idling on the approach. "I will run the winch. My truck, my winch."

"Fine," Tyler countered. "I've been out in the cold this long … I'll just stand here and freeze."

"The car is warm," Riley said reasonably. "Get in there and try to steer it while I work the winch." Riley's expression was gleeful as he dropped his voice to a conspiratorial level, "We'll let Matt stand out in the cold." Matt had wedged himself under the front bumper of the car to secure the clevis to the car's frame, so they could pull the vehicle out of the ditch without causing damage.

Tyler slipped behind the wheel of Chrissi's car and tried to concentrate on getting the vehicle out of the ditch. But his focus shifted unerringly to the documents he'd found on the floor in front of the passenger seat. What could the explanation be? It could be innocent; or it could be a secret. Tyler peered out the windshield at his best friend, Matt, Chrissi's brother. Something pulled deep inside, as he felt that Chrissi wouldn't want Matt to know about the documents. He gathered them, trying not to read the details, and folded the papers. Tyler slipped them inside his coat pocket. Whether there was a secret or not, that was her business. He would stay out of it. If the documents had an innocent explanation … he would be relieved. But Tyler feared that wasn't the case.

It didn't take long for the three men to get the car extracted from the snowy ditch and they were soon enjoying a hearty breakfast at the truck stop. "How's business?" Riley asked Matt as they ate.

Matt nodded and smiled as he swallowed a bite of eggs. "It's good. Finished up a job – got a couple more started and then there's a big one I'm waiting to hear back on my pitch," he answered. "Right now things are looking good." Matt's work as a sculptor had been growing in popularity and the demand had been increasing accordingly. Back when he began, Matt would often work part-time with either Riley at the metal fabrication company he had purchased about four years earlier, or with Tyler in the landscaping business. "You staying busy?" Matt countered.

"Couldn't be better," Riley confirmed. "Just hired a new guy … he's got an associate's degree, with a background in welding and design. He's already pushing me to update some of the equipment at the shop. Wants to do some laser work."

"You going to do it?" Tyler asked.

Riley pushed his empty plate aside. "I've got to consider it," he replied. "It would be nuts to ignore the idea." He leaned back against the backrest of the booth seat. "Besides … with Shelby back working at the Chronicle, there's a little more breathing room in the budget. It might be a good time to expand the business."

"How's it going at the newspaper?" Tyler asked. The question wasn't directed to anyone in particular, since Matt's wife, Ashley, was the new owner of the newspaper, and Riley's wife, Shelby, had recently become re-employed as a reporter and photographer.

"Good," came the reply. "Catherine and Charlie are eager to get through the transition and retire," Matt added. "Ashley's been putting in really long hours to get on top of the business side of things and covering her responsibilities on the reporting."

"What about Shelby?" Tyler asked. "I thought she was the reporter?"

"They share the reporting duties," Riley explained. "Shelby doesn't want to rely on Mom for babysitting too much for the twins, but she's eager to pull her weight at the paper, too. Sometimes she'll have Rori watch them, when she's not in school. Right now it's working really well." Rori, a sophomore at Miller's Bend High School, was the daughter of Riley's brother, Andrew.

Matt laughed. "I think those two women get competitive over any hard news that comes up," he said. "And they each seem to be possessive about their government boards – city council is Ashley's turf and the school board is Shelby's. When the commissioners meet, they both attend those meetings. It's kind of funny to watch."

"Maybe it's funny for you, but if you remember, Shelby was attacked after a school board meeting," Riley fumed. "Sure, you think it's a quiet little town – but just wait until somebody tries to hurt your woman."

"That had nothing to do with the school board," Tyler reminded them. "Could have happened anywhere. It was just lucky you were there to save her – she's forever in you debt," he joked.

"Ahh. Yes, she is," Riley countered with a sly smile. "Life is good."

"Sure is," Matt echoed.

Tyler rolled his eyes and sighed.

It seemed to be the cue to get back to their respective jobs and they rose to leave. "Hey, Tyler," a voice called from near the back of the café as they moved toward the exit. Tyler turned in response to see Erik Dunn, the sheriff, waving him over.

Tyler said good-bye to his friends and strode to the table where Erik was seated alone, pulled out a chair and sat. "What's up?" Tyler asked.

"Just wanted to thank you for calling in about the stranded car last night," the other man began. "I hate searching for missing people and notifying family members that we've found an abandoned vehicle. It gets them all upset," he added.

"And it's a waste of resources," Tyler contributed. "How's it going?"

"The job?" Erik asked. Seeing Tyler's nod, he continued, "It's good. Once you've been through the aftermath of your first fatality shoot-out, everything else is tolerable." Erik Dunn had only been on the job as the county sheriff a few months, and although he hadn't been in the room the day of the shooting, he had been working with Special Agent Stockard prior to the incident, and the man's death had impacted him profoundly. As the ranking local law enforcement official, Erik had worked with the state Division of Criminal Investigation and federal authorities following the shooting.

After a pause, Erik asked, "How's your dad?"

"He's good. Getting stronger every day," Tyler replied. He thought of the conversations the two had had the previous evening – the first with Chrissi present, and another, more emotional one when Tyler had returned home later. They'd finally agreed not to discuss the issue of Tyler's biological family further until they'd both had time to think it through.

"You think he'll come back? You know – as police chief?" Erik asked with a hint of trepidation. "He's a good man. And a good role model. Even though he's on the city police department and I'm in the county's sheriff's office, he has helped me a lot," he concluded.

Would Jeff return to his position in the police department? Tyler didn't know. "Guess we'll have to wait and see," he said noncommittally. "See ya' around," Tyler added as he rose to leave.

What a day! Chrissi rubbed the back of her neck as she glanced around the school parking lot in search of her car. The school secretary had told her that her brother had dropped off the keys in the morning with instructions to be sure Chrissi got them, but she wasn't having any luck locating the car. Maybe if she waited a few minutes for the traffic to clear, she'd see it more easily.

She sat on a cement bench – a really cold cement bench – in front of the school's main doors to wait. The day hadn't started well ... she'd overslept, then felt sick and couldn't eat breakfast. She'd barely been ready to go when Tyler picked her up to deliver her to the school. She got her make-up slip and headed to her classes only to discover pop-quizzes in two classes and a major chapter test in history. Oh sure, she'd known about the history test, but it had slipped her mind.

And she'd been worried about the papers from the doctor's office ... she couldn't find them in the apartment or in her bag. She must have left them in the car last night. And if Tyler had enlisted the help of Matt and Riley to free her snowbound car – which he clearly had, since it was Matt who had delivered it to the school – then Matt would have seen the papers. *This isn't going to go well. Not well at all.* She let her head droop forward into her hands.

"Hey, Chrissi?" a voice called softly. "Hey, are you okay?"

Chrissi looked up and found the cheerful face of Rori Wheeler. The girl was a couple of years younger and sort of a surrogate cousin … an unofficial relative due to the close friendship of Matt with Rori's Uncle Riley. They often found themselves at the same family gatherings and being nearer to the same age than anyone else, they had become friends.

Chrissi pulled deep for a smile she hoped was reassuring. "Yes, I'm fine." She stood and glanced again over the cars remaining in the parking lot and finally found her Grand Prix. Rori was still standing close, watching Chrissi intently.

"You're sure?"

Chrissi nodded. She was fine … at least until she talked with her mom, and Matt. And even though they would be upset, she knew deep down, that they loved her and would support her. Yes, she would be fine. "Do you need a ride?" she asked the younger girl. "I was just headed home. I can give you a lift."

Rori shook her head, declining the offer. She rubbed her hands down her denim-clad thighs and looked away as she answered, "A friend is picking me up." Just then a jacked-up pickup approached the curb and the driver laid on the horn. Rori startled and dashed for the passenger door. Chrissi's eyes narrowed as she watched her friend climb inside and the pair pull away from the school's entrance. She recognized that truck, and the driver – Adam Brewer. Nothing good could come of this.

CHAPTER FOUR

Shelby slipped quietly into the business office of The Chronicle, where her friend and boss, Ashley, was engrossed in compiling income and expense statements for the month. "Hey," Shelby began in a chipper voice. "You about ready to call it a day?"

As she looked up, Ashley pushed her red hair back from her face and sighed heavily. "May as well. Just let me print these reports and then I'll shut down." She tapped the keys to send the documents to print and then stood and stretched. She enjoyed owning the small-town newspaper. It was a nice change from the life she'd lived since college, traveling and working as a researcher for a major television news network.

By the time she collected the documents from the printer, slipped them into her bag and shut down her computer, Shelby had reappeared in the doorway. "Do you have time to grab a bite together, or do you need to hurry home?" Shelby asked her long-time friend.

She nodded. "I'd love that," she responded. "Matt's at the studio and he can get lost in his work for hours." They headed for the back exit, and Ashley paused, "Is the front door locked?"

Shelby replied that the receptionist, Bobbie, had assured her that she would lock it when she left. The two passed through and secured the back door while visiting. They walked the short distance to a little coffee shop, The Daily Grind, and claimed a table and ordered a large supreme pizza. Allison arrived moments after the two had settled, and they welcomed her warmly. Besides being friends, Shelby and Allison were also sisters-in-law, having married brothers Riley and Andrew Wheeler.

"Any news?" Allison asked teasingly as she glanced between her friends. With both of her best friends working in the local news industry, it was a safe opening question.

"Actually it's been kind of slow lately," Shelby responded. "We need some action in this town."

"Not hardly!" Ashley countered. "After covering the shooting – and the aftermath – I'm content with board meetings and social news!"

"But our readers aren't," Shelby replied. "We've got to dig up some gritty news … do some investigative reporting … uncover a big secret."

"In Miller's Bend? You've got to be kidding!" Allison laughed. "Thankfully, nothing exciting ever happens here."

Shelby reminded the two that when she'd arrived in Miller's Bend, a stalker had followed her to town and he'd attacked her. Riley had befriended Shelby when she'd first moved to the small town, but she'd tried to ignore her attraction to him. But as they got to know each other, he had grown protective of her, and ultimately saved her from the attacker.

Allison noted that she had come to town about a year later when she'd lost her job because of state budget cuts. She and her daughter, Hope, had stayed with Shelby and Riley during

Shelby's period of bed rest before the birth of the twins. Unknown to anyone, Lauren, the sister of Hope's deceased father had followed her to Miller's Bend with the intention of taking Hope. Thankfully, the loving network of friends and Mrs. Holmes had influenced Lauren and she'd become a helpful and loving component in Hope's life. She had dated Matt for a while, but returned to her home near Rapid City a few months later.

"Don't forget Andrew's troubles with his ex-wife," Ashley contributed. "Poor woman – Lucy sure had troubles."

Allison shivered. "Don't remind me. Who knows what would have become of our girls if Rori hadn't been so smart. She saved herself and Hope with her brave actions when Lucy took them."

"That crisis really locked you and Andrew together as a couple," Shelby pointed out. "We all knew you liked each other – a lot – but you were both scared to admit it before the girls were taken."

Allison nodded, her raven pony tail bobbing. "We were lucky to have Pastor Mark to counsel with," she acknowledged. "There were times that we would fall back into our patterns of distrust, but he helped us through them. And the girls have both counseled with him as well."

"Thankfully, you and Matt didn't have any danger and drama surrounding your courtship," Allison said to Ashley. "It was smooth sailing for you two."

Ashley snorted, "Unless you count the 'Chrissi' element."

"And the amnesia," Shelby reminded.

"Well, you recovered your memories, bought the Chronicle and Chrissi is home safe and sound," Allison countered. "Matt's mom's cancer is in remission, too."

With her optimistic outlook, Shelby summarized, "Well, we've all had our share of excitement. Maybe now things will settle down and be calm for a while."

"Right," Allison confirmed. "What could possibly happen that would compare?"

Her cell phone buzzed. No one spoke as their attention was drawn to the device.

Allison answered the call and listened a moment. She assured the caller that she would be right there and ended the conversation. "I've got to pick up Hope from OST," she said distractedly, referring to the school district's Out of School Time program. As a member of the pre-kindergarten class, Hope was eligible to be enrolled in OST on days when she didn't have class.

"I thought Rori was going to walk her home today," Shelby interjected. "What happened?"

"I don't know, but Rori didn't show up, and OST closed a few minutes ago," Allison explained. "See you guys later." And she was out the door.

"That's weird," Shelby commented. "Rori's always so reliable. I hope nothing's wrong."

The sun had long-since set and the sky had darkened by the time they finished off the pizza and paid the bill. Continuing to chat, the pair headed back toward their vehicles which were still parked near the Chronicle building. Ashley let her gaze slide over the two-story brick building and a sense of pride surged: It was hers and she was growing to love both the building and the business.

That's when she noticed a faint glow and movement through one of the side windows. "Did you see that?" she asked quickly.

She didn't wait for Shelby to reply, but dashed toward the front entrance. "Somebody's inside!" Shelby raced after her friend.

The door stood ajar and they burst through surprising a shadowy figure inside the office. Ashley automatically flipped the light switch, illuminating the front office. Instead of running past the two women toward the front door, the intruder fled toward the back of the building. Ashley's pulse hammered in her ears as she chased after the figure. "Ash, no!" Shelby called.

Shelby looked quickly around the front office and saw that the till stood open … empty. A crow bar lay near the safe and a computer had been smashed. She quickly dialed 911 to report the intruder as she dashed back out the main entrance. Peering around the corner of the building, she saw the side door fly open and the darkly dressed figure turned the corner before disappearing down the alley.

Ashley appeared at the back door, but broke off her pursuit. "You okay?" she called to Shelby, who responded with a thumbs up sign. They walked together to the mouth of the alley and looked the direction the intruder had disappeared. Silently they moved back to the rear entrance and stepped inside the building. "Don't touch anything," Ashley said quietly.

"I know. I've called the police," Shelby countered.

From the front office a voice called, "Hello?" It repeated quickly, "Hello? This is Sheriff Dunn. Anybody here?"

"We're in the back," Ashley answered as the two women moved through the dark corridor toward the front office.

The broad beam of a flashlight slashed through the darkness, illuminating a path for them. "You ladies alright?"

They heard sirens approaching the building as they stepped into the lighted office space. "We're fine," Ashley confirmed. "We scared the intruder away."

"But he emptied the till and destroyed at least one of the computers," Shelby added. She regarded Sheriff Dunn closely and then asked, "How'd you get here so fast? The city cops aren't even here yet."

"I was at the convenience store … less than two blocks away," he answered with a smile. "I figured if the intruder was still here, you could be in danger."

Dunn was a handsome man, and Shelby thought secretly, if she wasn't happily married, his charm would surely get her attention. Since he'd been elected as the county sheriff last November, he'd proven that he was good at his job. She'd seen him interact with children when he taught the Drug Abuse Resistance Education program at the local school and he related naturally with them. The DARE program had been nonexistent under the former sheriff's term.

She'd also seen the way he had worked with other law enforcement agencies, and was impressed with the way he worked as part of a team. As far as Shelby knew, he hadn't been dating anyone since moving to Miller's Bend. A fact Shelby vowed to help correct.

City police officer Josh Pendelton pushed open the antique door and joined the group in the office. "What are you doing here?" he asked as he glanced at the sheriff.

"I was just in the neighborhood …"

"Did you see the perp?" Pendelton asked, cutting off Dunn's response.

"Negative." The men eyed each other a moment and then Dunn shrugged. "Guess I'll follow the tracks, see where they end," he said. Turning his attention back to the women, he nodded and touched the brim of his hat, "Evening, ladies." And he left.

Before the door closed, Shelby heard Dunn's quiet words, "Hope your backup gets here soon."

With a scowl, Pendleton turned his attention back to Shelby and Ashley, "Did you touch anything?"

Ashley told the story, beginning with how she noticed movement and light in the window, and ending with Pendleton's arrival. She also related the fact that the invader had opened the back door to leave as if he knew that it didn't lock from the inside. "He didn't even slow down and consider how to get out," she said with conviction. "He's been here before and was confident that exit would work." She explained that the lock in the antique back door was always engaged from the outside, but never engaged from the inside. "You can't get locked in this building," she concluded.

"You're sure it was a man?" Pendleton asked.

Ashley shook her head. "No, I guess I just assumed ..."

"Shelby? Shelby!" The door flew open and Riley burst into the room. "What happened?" he demanded as he rushed to his wife. Holding her tightly, he added, "Are you alright?"

"Yes, I'm fine," she began. "There was a break-in."

Pendleton spoke into his radio, "Can I get some backup down at the Chronicle building? Now!" Then to himself, he muttered something about the whole town showing up to ruin his crime scene. He led Ashley away to continue questioning her about the intruder.

Holding Shelby at arm's length, Riley demanded more harshly than he'd intended, "Why didn't you answer your phone?"

"I'm sorry, Riley," she replied as she pulled the phone from her coat pocket. "Oh, it's set on silent, and in my coat, I guess I didn't feel it vibrate." Her forehead crinkled as she looked into Riley's worried eyes, "How did you even know anything was wrong?"

"Mom tried calling you, and when you didn't answer, she called me," he supplied calmly. "You were later getting home than you had told her, so she was worried." Riley's mother had been babysitting the twins, Jacob and Isabelle, as she graciously did most of the days Shelby worked.

"I told her it would be six today, and she was fine with that," Shelby answered, as she looked toward the clock. "Oh, gosh! I didn't realize it had gotten so late!"

"Exactly," Riley stated. "That's why I drove up here … I turned the corner onto Main Street and there are flashing lights all around the building. I about had a heart attack." He pulled Shelby into another quick hug.

"I'm sorry I worried you and your mom," Shelby replied. "I'll head home right away." She glanced toward Ashley and Officer Pendleton, and hesitated.

"It's okay," Riley said quietly. "I'll call Mom and tell her I'm on my way. I'll explain everything so she stops worrying. You help Ashley and then come home when you can."

Shelby's gratitude showed in her blue eyes as her gaze snagged on her husband's. She was so lucky to have the love of a man like Riley. "You're sure you're alright with that?" she asked.

"Absolutely," he asserted. "Just promise you'll be careful … leave at the same time and come straight home."

"I will," she said as she smiled up at him. "You're the best."

40

Sheriff Dunn returned in time to catch the Wheelers' heartfelt goodbye and felt a twinge of jealousy. He nodded as Riley passed him on his way out.

Pendleton and Ashley reappeared from the central part of the building and Pendleton looked disappointed that Dunn had returned. "Find anything?"

Dunn shook his head. "There were a few footprints, but vehicles have been driving through the alley and wiped most of them out. Where's your backup, Pendleton?"

Pendleton looked away from the scrutinizing gaze from Dunn. "I'll call dispatch again," he replied. "We're running a short roster tonight."

Dunn stepped closer and lowered his voice, "Why didn't you mention it? I could have had deputies down here to assist."

"I don't need your help," Pendleton snarled. "It's a break-in. The perp's gone. We'll never get him."

"Not with that attitude!" Dunn glared at the city law man. "Did you dust for prints? Ask neighboring business owners if they saw anything suspicious? Did you even notice that there was no forced entry?"

Pendleton's eyes widened and then narrowed dangerously. "This is my crime scene, Dunn. Butt out!"

Ashley cleared her throat loudly, drawing the attention of both men. With her brows raised she calmly said, "This is my business. And I want this burglary solved." She stepped forward, closer to the men who had been bickering and said, "I trust that you can put your differences aside in the interest of solving this crime and keeping the community safe."

Chagrined, both men nodded. "Absolutely," Dunn grunted.

Shelby spoke up, trying to move the investigation forward, so she could get home to her husband and children. "Did you say the intruder didn't force his way inside?" she asked, focusing on Dunn. "How …"

"I'd say either the person you saw had gotten a key somewhere," Dunn began.

"Or you left the door unlocked," Pendleton concluded as he examined the door and the door frame for damage.

Ashley and Shelby looked toward each other, and Ashley covered her face with her hands. "Bobbie. Bobbie said she'd lock the door and we never checked it," she exclaimed. "It's that simple. Someone came along and found the door open, slipped in and took the money from the till."

"I'm sorry to have caused so much trouble," she said, directing her comments to Pendleton. "All this … and there's a simple explanation."

Pendleton's smile oozed insincerity as he closed his notebook. "It's alright Mrs. Vander Meer. An occasional wild goose chase livens things up a bit. If you find any real crimes, be sure to call." As he turned to leave, Shelby opened her mouth to stop him, but a stern look from Dunn and a shake of his head stopped her.

"Good night, Pendleton," Dunn said as the other man reached for the door. Dunn quickly opened it for him, without touching the metal handle. "Sleep tight."

Pendleton wheeled to face Dunn. "Why don't you stay out of my city? You've got the whole county to patrol … I'm sure you've got better things to do than look over my shoulder."

"I can't wait until Chief Schuster is back on the force," Dunn retorted as he let the door fall closed behind the other man.

He sighed heavily and turned his attention back to the women. "Alright, Shelby. Let's hear what's on your mind," Dunn said.

"It's doubtful, Sheriff, that Pendleton's assumptions are correct," she said confidently. "The person who was in here was here with a purpose. He or she was dressed all in dark colors, had their face covered and," she paused to point to the floor near the safe, "they happened to be carrying a crow bar with them."

"What are the odds?" Ashley asked with sarcasm.

"Yeah, I know," Dunn answered. He'd noted the same details, plus, when he had walked down the alley, he had spoken with a worker from the nearby bar. The man had seen a person dressed in dark clothes run down the alley and jump into the passenger seat of a waiting pickup. From the description, Dunn figured he knew who the pickup belonged to – Adam Brewer.

The part of the story that had surprised him was that the driver had reportedly been a young teenage girl. That meant Brewer was likely the suspect in the break-in. But who was the girl? And did she realize she was an accomplice?

CHAPTER FIVE

Had it really been less than 48 hours since he had given Chrissi a ride into town after her car careened into the ditch? Tyler shook his head in disbelief. Yes, that was right – it had been Wednesday evening. He, Riley and Matt had pulled the car out Thursday morning and that's when Tyler had found the documents and tucked them into his coat pocket.

He needed to return them to Chrissi, but he hadn't had a chance. He hadn't seen her since he'd given her a ride to school Thursday morning before heading out to dislodge the car from the ditch. He'd been scheduled to work the noon to midnight shift on the ambulance, after which he'd crashed until mid-morning. By then Chrissi was back in class at the high school.

Now, as he sat at the table nestled in Mrs. Holmes' kitchen, her words really weren't registering with Tyler. She was chirping away about her husband, Harold, who had been deceased for more than a decade. Tyler let his mind wander as he picked at the cookies she'd laid before him and sipped at his hot chocolate. He thought he had timed his arrival to coincide with the time Chrissi should get back to her apartment in the afternoon, but she wasn't home yet. His thoughts were on Chrissi – and the documents he'd squirreled away to keep Matt from seeing. The desire to know what they said - what they *meant* - was formidable, but Tyler wouldn't stoop to reading them.

He had spent the early afternoon working in the greenhouse, transplanting seedlings of some varieties and planting seeds of others. When he'd purchased the stagnant business, the former owner had always ordered in and resold bedding plants over a short period each spring, but Tyler had a passion for growing the plants. So he had begun ordering seeds and planting them early … in January, February, and March. Some of the annual flowers grew slowly and required repeated transplanting and months of care before they were ready to sell. Tyler's business had expanded to include wholesale distribution of some seedlings to other greenhouses, rather than relying entirely on retail sales.

Mrs. Holmes' fragile hand was suddenly resting on Tyler's wrist. "What's possessed you?" she asked sharply.

Startled, Tyler's attention swung to the old woman. What had she been saying? "Uh, sorry. I guess my mind wandered," he responded quietly. "What were you -"

She flicked her hand in a dismissive gesture. "Never mind that – I was just reminiscing. What's got you so worried young man?" she asked.

Chrissi. My dad. My business, he thought, but Tyler didn't say the words. He shook his head and picked up a cookie. "Thanks for the treats," he said instead. "What are the Red Hatters up to these days?" he asked, referring to the club whose membership included a group of socially active "older women".

"Oh, there's nothing new there," she replied. The ancient wisdom behind Mrs. Holmes' intense scrutiny made Tyler wince. She wasn't about to be sidetracked that easily. "Now, go

46

ahead and tell me what's bothering you. You know it lightens the load if you share it with someone who loves you."

And Tyler had long ago recognized that Mrs. Holmes did love him … and his friends. He secretly suspected that he was the favored of the group she referred to as "my boys", and when he was younger he had wished with all his heart that she was his grandmother. He'd shared so much with her, especially when he was struggling to grow up.

He stalled as he debated whether to open up again.

"Do you remember the artwork you boys painted on my garage when you were just pups?" she asked mildly.

Tyler nodded. He remembered well. He and Riley had started it after school one spring day when they were young teens, rebellious and defiant. Tyler never knew why Riley wanted to do such a thing, as for himself, being the son of the town's police chief had a stigma. He was considered a goody, goody – a straight arrow – and he'd wanted to show his peers that he could be bad. So he'd bought a bunch of spray paint and he and Riley had set out to deface something. The first of several problems was that they didn't dare vandalize public property, and they didn't really want to be caught in the act. So they'd scouted around town and picked the wall of the detached garage belonging to the crazy old lady on the edge of town.

They didn't have much of a start on their "street art", Tyler remembered, when the new kid in town happened along – and had the obnoxious nerve to laugh at them. They'd roughed him up a bit for that, but he'd stood up to them. Before moving to Miller's Bend, the new kid – Matt Vander Meer – had lived in a city and had seen real graffiti. He'd probably even created some before, judging by the way he'd taken over their project.

They'd eventually given up and watched as Matt's work came to life before their eyes.

"Remember how that decision, that act, changed your lives?" Mrs. Holmes asked. "You got in trouble, didn't you?"

"Oh, yeah," Tyler replied as he remembered the incident. "Dad was torqued."

"To be sure," the old woman confirmed. "I was none too pleased with you all," she added with a smile. "I thought you were a herd of ruffians."

"It did change our lives, though," Tyler repeated her words. "Riley and I got to be even closer friends and we got to be friends with Matt while we served our sentence."

"You spent that summer painting my house," Mrs. Holmes reminisced. "It was a grand summer."

"We've painted it a couple of times since, too," he reminded her.

"Yes, it was my lucky day," Mrs. Holmes said with a hint of sadness. "I don't know how I'd have gotten by all these years without you boys, and Andrew, too," she said, referring to Riley's brother. "It truly was a blessing to me that you chose my garage to vandalize that day."

Tyler nodded and squeezed the hand of the woman who had served as a grandmotherly figure in his life … listening, guiding, helping and loving him when he had felt lost and alone. She was right, he reflected, a bad decision had turned out to be a blessing many times over for both him and her. God does work in mysterious ways.

"Now." She spoke with authority, "Tell me what's bothering you young man."

Tyler searched her features for a moment. He'd thought she was old when they were kids, but looking at Mrs. Holmes today, he realized that she had been old and now she was … ancient. Her skin had lost all hint of rosiness, and was paper thin, her muscle withered away, her hair white. She'd been such a steady part of his life that he hadn't considered that a day would come when she wouldn't be there for him – until this moment. He couldn't burden her with his concerns. "Are you feeling alright?" he asked.

Her pale silvery-grey eyes brightened and she pulled herself taller in her chair. "Of course I'm alright. You are the one who needs help," she quipped. "Now, out with it," she demanded.

"It's the secrets," he confided as he let his shoulders droop.

"What secrets?" she countered. Her scrutiny and her caring were too much, and Tyler looked away. His focus shifted around the room and he cleared his throat.

"I've lived my life believing one set of facts," Tyler explained as he trained is gaze on the window above the sink. "And suddenly I discovered that one fact is wrong – is a lie – and the other facts all fall into question. And the person who knows the answers is protecting the secrets."

Tyler paused, expecting to hear reassuring words from Mrs. Holmes. Perhaps a tale from the old days, a story from her own life, or even an adaptation of the verse from Proverbs, saying, a gossip betrays a confidence, but a trustworthy person keeps a secret. But she didn't speak.

Concerned, Tyler turned to the woman he had admired for so long, and her stunned expression told him in an instant that she knew exactly what he was referring to. The knife of betrayal sliced into his spirit as he realized the two most important people in his life had each, independently, or both in cooperation, kept the truth from him for nearly three decades.

Her complexion had gone from pale to sheet-white; she'd opened her mouth as if to speak, but gasped. And then, as Tyler watched, horrified, Mrs. Holmes wilted, falling forward against the table. Personal feelings pushed aside, Tyler immediately sprang to her side, easing her to the floor.

Even as he felt for a pulse, he pulled his cell phone from his jeans pocket and quickly pressed the keypad for emergency assistance. He ordered an ambulance while relating the patient's status. Initially he hadn't been sure if it was a simple faint, or stroke or heart attack. But Mrs. Holmes hadn't regained consciousness by the time he'd finished the call, increasing the probability that her condition was very serious.

She was breathing on her own, but her heart rate was weak and irregular. While he waited for the ambulance, Tyler covered her with a blanket and then held her hands and recited the Twenty-third Psalm for her peace of mind.

As soon as the ambulance arrived and the EMTs began to assess Mrs. Holmes, Tyler stepped back. His mind blanked as his eyes took in the scene. Twice now, within months, Tyler had been forced to watch helplessly as others took care of people he loved, working to save their lives. He held the door open as they wheeled Mrs. Holmes out to the waiting ambulance. And he watched dumbly as they loaded her on the gurney into the state-of-the-art vehicle.

One EMT would ride in the back, monitoring the patient until they reached the hospital. The other, a man Tyler had known for years, closed the door and then turned to Tyler. "You want to ride along?" he asked.

Tyler considered the offer only a few seconds before shaking his head in denial. "No," he croaked. "You'd better hurry."

CHAPTER SIX

Tyler didn't watch as the ambulance pulled away. He turned and slipped back into the kitchen. Numbly he slid into a chair. He heard the retreating sirens. Nausea sickened his stomach, his hands shook, his head throbbed and perspiration broke out across his brow.

Instinctively, Tyler curled forward in the chair, propping his elbows on his knees, cradling his head in his hands. He breathed deeply to try to calm himself. As an EMT, Tyler had been involved in far more traumatic scenes than the one just played out, but he'd never reacted this way.

Fear for Mrs. Holmes' health was at the forefront of his emotions, but he also couldn't ignore the fact that it had been his quest for information which had triggered her attack. And the certainty that she had known about his past raised more questions. How many people knew about the private adoption? Who was involved? And most importantly, was there a chance that Tyler had blood relatives in Miller's Bend?

Tyler realized that even though his mind had been occupied with sorting through facts and theories, his heart had been praying. His faith was strong, and relying on the Lord was a natural reaction. Asking for the healing care for Mrs. Holmes was obvious, but Tyler became aware that even in crisis, his prayer had expanded to include Chrissi, and his father.

"Ty?" A soft voice broke into his thoughts. And again it spoke, closer to him now. "Ty? What happened?" It was Chrissi's voice – a voice that vibrated with apprehension – that pulled him up out of the chair, up out of his thoughts. He turned to face her without the time or instinct to hide his emotions and instantly she was in his arms. She gave comfort and support, while asking nothing in return.

Thankfully, she didn't ask any more questions. She just held him and waited. He had yearned to hold Chrissi for so long, and now through a nasty twist of events, he had just what he wanted. The feel of holding her in his arms was inexplicably good, not just physically, but mentally and emotionally. He'd been angry and confused since the shooting, and being around Chrissi helped. Spending time with her helped. But holding her was like a piece of heaven. It soothed him. It quieted his soul.

Eventually, Tyler had to release Chrissi and she eased back, far enough to peer into his eyes. Her concern touched his heart. "I met the ambulance a little ways down the street. Did Mrs. Holmes fall or something?" she asked quietly.

Tyler twisted away, turning his back to Chrissi, shoving his hand through his dark wavy hair in aggravation. "Yah. Or something," he answered harshly.

Chrissi's pulse raced as she waited for Tyler to explain. She'd grown to know the man before her very well in her lifetime, and they'd become especially close in recent months. Whatever happened here today was far more than a medical emergency requiring the ambulance. Tyler was extremely close to Mrs. Holmes, but something here today had torn into his emotional core.

Waiting and watching Tyler as he battled some unknown internal quandary proved to be difficult, so Chrissi began picking up in the kitchen. She put away the milk and the chocolate flavoring powder; found a zipper bag and put the uneaten cookies in it; rinsed the cups and plates, and she wiped down the counters. She was just drying her hands, when Chrissi heard Tyler's quiet raggedly whispered statement. "She knew."

Unsure what he was referring to, she turned and found that Tyler had moved nearer to her. His expression was unshielded, and he looked so young and vulnerable that her heart ached. "What?" she asked. "She knew what?"

"All these years … I would run here – to Mrs. Holmes when I was lost or scared or alone," he explained quietly. "And all the time, she knew I was adopted, too. And she never told me."

Tyler watched as Chrissi's dark eyebrows drew low over her expressive eyes. "She couldn't have known," she countered. "Your dad said it was a private adoption between him and his wife, one of your birth relatives and an old lawyer."

Something dark surged in Tyler's expression. "I'm telling you – she knew!" Suddenly the emotional hurt was back in his voice as he continued. "I was waiting for you to come home and visiting with her. She kept asking me what was bothering me."

Chrissi's heart caught on Ty's words: he'd been waiting for her to come home … he'd wanted to see her! If it hadn't been for Mrs. Holmes medical emergency and Tyler's emotional whirlpool, Chrissi would be rejoicing over that tidbit. But the seriousness of the situation pushed that fact to the background.

"I didn't want to come right out and tell her that I was adopted," Tyler continued. "I talked about going through life believing one thing and then finding out that the people I love and trust have been lying to me. And how that makes me question everything," he said as he paced. "That's when she had her attack."

The meaning of what Tyler was saying struck Chrissi with an almost physical impact. He had been injured far worse by the deception surrounding his adoption, than he had been by the fact that he was adopted. The sense of betrayal he felt because the situation had been kept a secret was the stressful, painful factor in this situation.

And Chrissi had a secret, too. A sickening feeling swept over her as she reached for a chair. Sinking into it, she instinctively pulled one of the cookies from the zipper bag and bit into it, barely chewing and swallowing it. The sweetness of the morsel was vile, and almost immediately she knew that her stomach would reject it. Chrissi dashed to the bathroom, where she vomited, and cleaned up.

Moments later, she stepped out of the small room to find Tyler hovering nearby. Worry etched in his expression, he immediately stepped to her side and wrapped his arm around her waist. Her body stiffened at his touch and her breath caught, but she didn't pull away. "Everything okay?" he asked as he guided her back toward the kitchen.

She nodded mutely.

"You're sure?" he asked again as he walked her past the table and chairs in the kitchen, toward the exit.

She couldn't lie to him, but the whole truth seemed out of place at the moment. "I'll be just fine," she finally said.

Chrissi's behavior troubled Tyler, but he was glad that she hadn't pulled away when he'd held her after she came out of the bathroom. Maybe she just hadn't noticed yet. He snagged Chrissi's backpack as they passed through the kitchen. They left the main floor of the Victorian home and moved to the entrance to Chrissi's basement apartment. A narrow stairway descended to the living area and Tyler was forced to let go of the hold he had on Chrissi.

Reluctantly, he pulled his hand away from her slender waist, but claimed her hand as he led the way down the steps. He didn't want her to fall, and she might be lightheaded after the incident upstairs. And he liked the feel of her hand in his. He liked the feel of her spirit in his life.

They entered the apartment, still holding hands, and as she began to move toward the kitchen counter, Tyler gently pulled her back toward him. She turned in response to his tug, and smiled. Her eyes were tired and her smile seemed frail.

She should be full of life and vitality, Tyler thought, not exhausted and worried. "Are you sure you're alright?" he queried for a third time. "Tell me what's going on, Chris," he pleaded, stepping close and wrapping her in his embrace. The tenderness in his voice was too much for Chrissi when Tyler quietly whispered in her ear, "Let me help."

Rooted to the spot, Chrissi was aware of her apprehension as Tyler slid his hands to her arms and traced the outline of her shoulders and neck until his hands cupped her face and she was compelled to raise her gaze to meet his. A single tear escaped and slipped silently onto her cheek – a fact that she was unaware of until Tyler's lips gently kissed it away.

Chrissi's heart soared. How many times had she wished in her naïve dreams that Tyler would see her as a woman? How many times had she planned her reaction and hoped that their friendship would change, grow and evolve into more?

Just as gently as the first kiss had been, a second kiss brushed her other cheek. And then, a touch to her lips brought reality back. Tension coiled through her in reaction to the intimate touch and Chrissi remembered that this dream would not be. Things had happened, events that had changed her life and the possibilities for her. She couldn't let Tyler care more about her without knowing what the new truth was. She would have to tell him – she owed him that much.

The sick feeling was beginning to rise again. It started as heat in her stomach and she knew that in minutes she would be retching again if she didn't eat something. She couldn't look at Tyler as she pulled away and stepped to the kitchen counter.

Silently he watched as she filled a glass with lukewarm water and snatched a couple of crackers from a nearby package that lay open on the counter top. Pain stabbed at his core as Tyler added these facts to his suspicions. He wanted to know the truth. But he didn't want to know the truth.

"Chris …," he began to ask her what was going on, but his voice broke. Maybe she'd tell him in her own time. And maybe she wouldn't. But he decided not to ask.

She'd downed two crackers and pulled a couple more from the package. "What?" she asked automatically when he didn't continue to speak.

Tyler glanced around the apartment. Not many high school seniors lived on their own, even if they were over the age of 18, as Chrissi was. The question slipped out before Tyler realized he was about to ask it. "Why do you live here?"

She looked away, toward the little basement window above the couch. A stiff shrug lifted her shoulder as she responded, "Rent's cheap."

"No, Chris," Tyler said as he stepped closer to her again. "Why do you have an apartment? Why aren't you at home?"

She explained that although she, Matt and their mother, Melanie, had all lived together in Melanie's house, they'd recently split up. When Matt and Ashley got married, Melanie had gifted the house to them and taken an apartment for herself. Chrissi hadn't wanted to live with the newlyweds. And Melanie's apartment was in the same complex with her ex-husband, Byron, who was also Chrissi's father. Chrissi had been certain that Melanie and Byron were trying to rebuild their relationship after a 16 year absence on Byron's part. Chrissi hadn't wanted to be underfoot. And, she'd said, she reached a point where she needed more privacy.

Tyler listened. It made perfect sense. And, because Chrissi was legally an adult it wasn't unreasonable at all. "Do you have a … a boyfriend?" he asked and instantly wished he hadn't.

"No," she answered with a small smile. Then her eyes met Tyler's and she understood the real question. *Are you sleeping with someone?* He didn't speak the words, but she read the question in his face. "No," she repeated. "Mrs. Holmes would never stand for anything like that, and, anyway … I wanted to save that for marriage."

Wanted, Tyler repeated in his mind. Past tense. Once again words escaped before he caught himself. "Tell me what happened in Chicago. Please?" He had a sick feeling that he knew, at least part of it.

"I can't," she whispered brokenly. He'd moved closer to her again. She met his gaze and repeated, "I can't make myself say it out loud."

Tyler wrapped her in his arms, holding, rocking, soothing and assuring her that everything would be okay, as she cried. He still didn't know details, but his suspicions were growing. And in spite of it all, Tyler's determination to help Chrissi deepened. He had some soul searching to do, but he wasn't about to leave her to navigate through her distress alone.

Finally, her tears dried up, and she tried to apologize.

Tyler silenced her by touching a forefinger to her lips. "I'm the one who's sorry, Chris. I shouldn't have pushed you," he said. "If you're ever ready to tell me, I'll listen. If you're never ready to tell me, I'll still be here for you."

The silence that stretched between them was broken by the ringtone of Tyler's cell phone. He answered briskly, as though the call was in annoyance, but then listened to the caller several minutes before replying with a clipped "Okay" and ending the call. Chrissi searched his face for a clue as to the content of the call. He was agitated, and had begun pacing and pushing his hand through his hair as he'd listened to the caller.

Chrissi didn't know whether his actions were in response to the call or to their conversation. Her mind had been busily trying to process what had just happened between her and Tyler. Did he know? Had he guessed? Did what happen in Chicago really not matter to him? It couldn't be that easy.

"That was the hospital," he began absently. "Mrs. Holmes has been admitted. She's stable but unconscious. And apparently I need to sign some paperwork."

"Why?" Chrissi asked as she moved to his side. "Is she going to be okay?"

"I don't know," he grated out in response. "I don't know *anything!*"

"You'd better go to her," Chrissi replied.

Tyler didn't move away from Chrissi. Instead, he tenderly cupped her cheek, his eyes searching hers. Ever so slowly, he lowered his head, and very lightly kissed her lips. He felt her tremble, but she didn't pull away. "I'd better go," he whispered. "If you need anything, you'll call me?"

Chrissi nodded as her throat constricted. She heard his steps as Tyler headed up the stairs to the exit. The door closed. His pickup started up. And he drove away.

Cadee Brystal

CHAPTER SEVEN

The Wheeler family celebrated some odd traditions, Chrissi thought as she sat quietly in the family room, listening to Riley's and Andrew's father, Lawrence, tell stories from his youth. Lawrence and his wife, Beth, had begun the tradition of hosting a fish fry for their family and friends on a Sunday in late March. Beth explained that it was a good way to purge the freezer of the fillets of walleye and perch amassed during the winter ice fishing season, before the spring season opened again in April.

In contrast to the early days of the event when only the four Wheelers were there, the fish fry had blossomed. Today the guests included Riley and Shelby, and their two-year-old twins, Jacob and Isabelle; Andrew and Allison, with Rori and Hope; Matt and Ashley; Chrissi; their parents, Melanie and Byron; Tyler and his father, and Erik Dunn. Mrs. Holmes would have been included, but she remained hospitalized.

The women, Lawrence and Jeff were visiting in the family room, while the other men prepared the meal. Lawrence was telling in extreme detail the story about the time his brother had shot the bucket of eggs as he'd toted it from the hen house to their aunt's kitchen door. "Lucky he was a lousy shot,"

Lawrence laughed at the conclusion, "If he'd have hit me, like he intended …"

Chrissi was uncomfortable and to compound that, the smells wafting through the house had begun to make her feel queasy again. Maybe if she nibbled on a slice of bread, it would help.

Restlessly, she wandered to the kitchen where the guys were enjoying friendly banter as they cooked. She sidled past Erik and Matt before Tyler noticed her approach, he glanced up and smiled, but didn't say anything. They hadn't talked since the evening in her apartment, and she wasn't really sure where they stood. She turned away, reaching for the handle of the cupboard door.

"Hey! No snacking!" Byron ordered, startling Chrissi. She turned quickly to face him and her skin flushed as if caught doing something wrong. Byron, her father, had reentered their lives only recently and had been trying to fit in, but he instantly knew he had embarrassed her and he tried to cover it up. "Sorry, honey. Go ahead, if you can't wait."

She didn't move, and didn't know what to say. Chrissi just stood there registering the questioning looks she was getting from the guys. Her brain stalled and she felt the panic rise as the seconds ticked by.

Then Tyler was in front of her, smiling, blocking the view of the others. "You need some snacks for the twins? I'll bet they're getting restless aren't they?" Relieved, she nodded. She turned again toward the cupboard, as Tyler reached past her and pulled down a box of crackers. "Here," he said as he placed the box into her hands. "These should help." She smiled, whispered a soft thank you and quickly left the kitchen.

They dined in two shifts with the women and children eating first, while the men continued to cook. And then the men took their turn eating while the women began the clean-up process. Chrissi and Rori took Hope, Isabelle and Jacob outside for a walk around the Wheeler farm. It was still cold and the wind was sharp, but the sun's rays were beginning to warm the earth. The children ran ahead as Chrissi and Rori strolled toward the barn.

Delighted squeals reached their ears as the children began capturing and petting the barn cats. Beth enjoyed the cats, not quite to the point of being a "crazy cat lady", but made sure to feed them at the barn so they wouldn't become nuisances around the front door of the house. The cats, which came in an array of colors, were healthy and tame. An old Border collie named Pal trotted along behind the teenage girls.

They walked in silence until they reached the doorway of the barn where they stopped. Standing in the sunlight, rather than going on inside, they could enjoy the warmth of the rays, and still watch the little kids. The two hadn't talked since Chrissi had seen Rori jump into Adam's pickup. Rori seemed to sense what Chrissi planned to say and the younger girl turned away as she drew in a deep breath.

"Rori ... about Adam ..." Chrissi began only to be cut off by a glare from Rori. Her deep brown eyes seemed to burn with a rare fury as she faced her older friend.

"I don't want a lecture," Rori hissed. "I can make my own decisions."

Chrissi drew back, as if she'd been slapped, but recovered quickly. "Don't snap at me. I'm your friend," she retorted. Stepping closer and lowering her voice so Hope wouldn't overhear, Chrissi added, "If you think you're old enough to make your own decisions, at least make intelligent ones."

"And you think Adam's a bad decision?" Rori countered. "How Christian of you to judge him," she added sarcastically.

Chrissi was stung by Rori's attitude. But she rallied quickly, "This isn't about me judging him. It's about the facts. Adam is bad news and I don't want you added to the trail of young girls he uses and discards."

"He just hasn't met the right girl yet," Rori argued. "Nobody understands him."

"Plenty of people understand him, Rori. But *you* don't," Chrissi pressed. "He picks up young girls and makes them feel 'special' until he gets them into bed and then he dumps them," she continued as her voice rose in both volume and pitch. "It's illegal, Rori. It's called statutory rape."

Rori blanched and looked into Chrissi's face. "I'm not dumb enough to sleep with him," she said flatly. "I just want to have a little fun."

"Well, I'm sure that's all he wants, too," Chrissi hissed as tears began to slide down her cheeks. "I'm sure a twenty year old man just wants to 'have a little fun' with a fifteen-year-old girl." She was shaking now, and struggling to stay calm. She grabbed Rori's hands and pleaded, "For heaven's sake, stay away from him. Please!"

"Potty?" a small voice broke into the conversation and Chrissi glanced down. Isabelle looked up at her and repeated, "Potty!"

"I got you, sweetie," Rori said as she reached down and picked the toddler up. "You have the other two?" she asked Chrissi before heading back to the house. Chrissi watched Rori and Isabelle hurrying away. She said a little prayer that her words would help Rori realize the dangers of hanging around with Adam and guys like him.

She was shivering by the time she persuaded Hope and Jacob to put the kitties back to bed and head into the house again. They stepped in through the entryway and as Chrissi helped the kids take off their coats and boots, she heard the conversation among the adults at the table. Shelby and Ashley were talking about a break-in at the newspaper office Thursday evening. Ashley told about how they had surprised an intruder and the person had fled through the back door.

As Chrissi pulled up a chair to join the group, Shelby asked Erik, who had apparently responded to their call to 911, whether there were any leads. He shook his head in a negative response as he swallowed a sip of coffee and returned the mug to a coaster. "There were no finger prints on the crow bar – and so many prints in the front office that they are no help. I thought that Adam Brewer might be involved, but I interviewed him and he swears he was at home," Erik said with a disbelieving smirk. "His mom backs him up on it, so I guess unless someone else can place him near the newspaper office Thursday, he's off the hook."

Chrissi's focus shot to Rori, who sat stiffly nearby, but hadn't said a word as she listened. Their gazes locked and Chrissi narrowed her eyes, willing Rori to say something. She read guilt in her friend's expression before it was replaced with silent defiance. Rori turned away.

While Chrissi and Rori silently battled over the ethics of keeping quiet, when she knew where Adam had been, the conversation continued without anyone noticing their exchange.

"Brewer?" Ashley repeated the name. "Why does that sound familiar?" she asked as she glanced around the table. Ashley had only been living in Miller's Bend a few months, and had been remarkably adept at learning people's names, but it could take years to make all the connections.

"He's in the court news a lot," Erik contributed. "One of these days he's going to get himself into trouble that his daddy can't get him out of."

"His father is a big-wig at the cheese plant. His step-dad runs a heating and cooling business," Beth contributed. "And his mother works for you," she added with a glance toward Ashley.

Erik and Ashley both stared at Beth. Erik was the first to connect the dots. "So he had access to a key?" he asked in dismay. "That's a whole new piece of the puzzle."

"His mom works for me? You mean Bobbie?" Ashley asked.

Erik's focus snapped to Shelby, "Wasn't Bobbie the one who supposedly locked the door that night?"

Shelby nodded in response.

"Well," Erik said with a grin. "Looks like I've got more work to do."

Chrissi didn't say anything, but rose and walked toward the other room. She thumped Rori on the head, in a loving, sisterly way, as she passed by.

"Hey!" Rori called after her. "What was that for?"

Chrissi glanced back over her shoulder. "Intelligent decisions."

Citing the need to finish her homework, Chrissi prepared to leave the gathering soon afterward. She thanked Riley's parents, and as she buttoned her jacket, she bid goodbye to all and left the house. Her car's motor was running and the interior was warm – someone had slipped out of the house and started it for her. And her missing documents lay on the seat. She glanced around, thinking that whoever had returned them would want to talk to her about their meaning … about her pregnancy. But no one was in sight.

She sighed. It had to be Matt. But why hadn't he mentioned it? She would have to drive over to the house and talk to him. Maybe tonight … or maybe tomorrow night. How long could she avoid it?

Tyler watched as Chrissi drove away. Maybe he should have told her that he'd had the documents and that he'd been the one who had placed them back on her passenger seat. But she had to have known it was him, right? And he didn't want to pressure her to discuss it, not after he'd promised that he wouldn't. This was probably for the best. Probably.

Riley was seated at the dining table supervising the twins as they had a late afternoon snack, as Chrissi had made her departure. He watched as his wife, who had been gazing out the window, turned to Erik and said, "Isn't she something?"

"Ah, Shelby?" Riley called to her, but it was too late.

"Who?" Erik responded carefully, "Chrissi?"

"Shelby, honey," Riley attempted to gain Shelby's attention.

"Of course, Chrissi," she replied sweetly, ignoring her husband. "She's the only eligible woman here," she added with a brilliant smile.

"Not for me, thanks," Erik replied as he stepped toward the closet to retrieve his coat.

"Shelby!" Riley tried again to intervene. She shot him a dark glare.

"She's per-fect," Shelby sing-songed to Erik's back.

"She's ta-ken," Erik echoed in reply.

And the whole house went quiet – even the twins stopped squirming and stared at Erik.

Matt's voice cut through the silence. "What?!"

Erik glanced around at the faces staring at him. "What? You mean nobody noticed -"

"I'd guess it's time to head back to town," Jeff said as he pushed himself up out of the recliner he'd been enjoying. "I believe Tyler went out to start the truck, I'd best get out there or I'll be walking home." Erik passed Jeff's coat to him, but didn't say a word as the two exited the house.

As soon as the door closed behind them, Erik turned to Jeff. "What just happened in there?"

"I'd say you let the cat out of the bag," Jeff responded as he kept walking toward the truck.

"Hold on," Erik called as he reached for the older man's shoulder. "You mean to tell me nobody knew?"

Jeff snorted. "Well, I knew. And I'd guess that Riley knew, or he wouldn't have been trying to get Shelby's attention. But I reckon you kinda surprised the rest of 'em."

Jeff climbed into the passenger seat of the waiting truck, as Tyler glanced past him. "Why's everybody leaving at once?" he asked as he surveyed the trail of friends leaving the Wheeler house and heading for their vehicles.

"Might have been something Dunn said," his father replied as he settled into the seat and secured his seat belt.

Tyler shifted the truck into gear and smiled. "Looks like teenagers leaving a party when you'd show up … you know, back in the day," he said to his father. He shifted up through the gears before Tyler finally asked, "What did he say anyhow?"

"Oh, nothing much," Jeff countered. "Just didn't take Shelby up on her match-making attempt … seein' as how Chrissi is already taken."

Tyler stared hard at his father, who seemed to be enjoying the situation just a little too much. "What?" he croaked as they cruised down the highway.

Jeff laughed in response. "Eyes on the road, son. We don't want to die before you get this all straightened out," he advised. "Eyes on the road."

Cadee Brystal

CHAPTER EIGHT

After classes Monday, Chrissi swung by the track coach's office to tell her that she wouldn't be participating on the team this season. She gathered her things and headed for her car. The squeal of tires on pavement drew her attention and she glanced toward the source. Adam Brewer's pickup roared away from the curb where he usually picked up his quarry. There stood Rori, head hung low, swiping angrily at her cheeks.

With a sigh, Chrissi changed paths to offer comfort to her young friend. "Hey, Rori," she said quietly as she drew near. "Let me give you a ride?"

Rori glanced around quickly to see who else had noticed her standing there, humiliated. No one was looking her way and her gaze returned to Chrissi. "He's a jerk," she said quietly. Chrissi agreed and slung an arm around Rori's shoulders, as they headed toward her car.

"Come on, hon," Chrissi said sympathetically, "You don't need him."

"I know," she confirmed. "I told him I wasn't going to hang with him anymore and he got really mad." Chrissi unlocked the car doors and the two were stowing their backpacks when the pickup roared past, with the driver yelling insults at Rori.

"Get in! Quick!" Chrissi commanded. She dialed the sheriff's office to report the incident and then disconnected the call. Turning to face Rori, she spoke quietly, "I'm glad you decided to stay away from Adam. But if you know anything about him breaking in at the newspaper office, you have to tell Sheriff Dunn."

Rori's color drained from her face and she turned to look out the back window as the pickup stopped behind the red car. Chrissi hit the button to lock the car doors, sensing more trouble. Adam leaped out of the idling vehicle and slammed his fist on the trunk of Chrissi's car. "Are you nuts?" Rori replied to the idea of turning Adam in.

Adam continued to pound on the vehicle, cursing and yelling at the girls until his body was suddenly slammed down against the surface of the car's trunk. Sheriff Dunn hand-cuffed the man and stuffed him into a waiting suburban before he strode to the driver's side door and tapped on the window.

"I'll need you girls to come over to the office and give me a statement about what happened here, or I can't charge him with anything," Dunn said matter-of-factly. "And since you are a minor, you'll need to bring a parent, too," he added as he looked at Rori.

Rori nodded in resignation. "I'll call Dad and have him meet us there," she said.

One of the body shop's trucks came and loaded Adam's pickup to take it to the county impound.

It was after five o'clock when Chrissi got back to her apartment. She was exhausted and sad and worried about Rori. The girl had given the sheriff a lot more information about Adam and his behavior, including her knowledge about the break-in at the newspaper. Apparently, Rori had been driving his truck when he fled from the building. She was in big trouble with both the law, and with her parents. And Adam, if he found out she'd talked.

Chrissi popped some leftover casserole, brought over by Tyler on one of his visits, into the microwave and changed into some lounge pants and a loose T-shirt. She opened her laptop and her advanced biology textbook, and was about to take a bite of her supper, when she heard a knock on her apartment door.

Groaning inwardly, she laid the fork down on her plate and trotted up the steps to answer the door. She easily saw through the window that her visitor was her sister-in-law, Ashley. Smiling, Chrissi welcomed the other woman inside. "I hope this isn't a bad time," Ashley was saying as soon as they had descended the steps and entered the apartment. "I'd thought we could have a bite together," she explained as she indicated the container she carried, "but I see you're already eating."

"I was just about to start in when you knocked," Chrissi said a little self-consciously. "There's plenty. You're welcome to join me."

Their friendship was just beginning to take root and grow. Chrissi hadn't met Ashley until the day she returned from Chicago and by then the woman had become a very important part of Matt's life. She'd been in the interrogation room during the shooting, and had helped sooth Chrissi, when Matt's and Tyler's efforts had only heightened her fears. Chrissi had sensed that Ashley understood her reactions, and the beginning bonds of their relationship were woven in that moment.

"That'll work," Ashley replied as she turned to place the container into the refrigerator. "I'll just leave this and you can enjoy it another day," she added as she closed the door. "Fried chicken ... I made too much."

"Thank you," Chrissi whispered as she felt tears building in her eyes. "That's very kind."

"No problem. I remember living on canned soup and cheap noodles when I was in college," Ashley answered dismissively. "Enjoy some home cooking while you can."

They quickly consumed the casserole and Ashley asked for the recipe. "I don't have it," Chrissi confessed. In response to a questioning glance from her guest, she explained, "A friend brought it over … they had too much food and he …"

"He?"

Chrissi felt her cheeks heat with what she was sure was a rich, vibrant blush and willed the response to stop. "Just a friend …"

"A good friend?" Ashley asked, accentuating the question with a playful wink. "Or a boyfriend?"

Chrissi didn't respond, but felt the heat in her cheeks intensify and her ears burned. Boyfriend? Dumfounded, Chrissi stared into Ashley's face. What could she say? Nothing.

Before she realized what was happening, Ashley had pulled her into a tight hug, and whispered, "Matt knows."

"What? He knows what?" Chrissi asked warily. She had deduced that Matt would have figured out that she was pregnant, after reading the papers she had carelessly left in the car the night she'd slid into the ditch. However, she was cautious about discussing the situation with Ashley. They seemed to be forging a friendship, but …

A sly smile warmed Ashley's features. "Your little secret, of course," she chirped as she began gathering her coat and bag. "Matt was a bit startled at first," she confided. "But he's accepting it, now that he's had time to digest it."

"And he told you?"

Ashley nodded enthusiastically as she began making her way up the steps to the exit. "It's just so exciting! Even your parents are accepting the idea."

"My parents?" Chrissi questioned with some alarm as she trailed her sister-in-law. "He told my parents?!"

"Oh, don't be silly, he didn't tell them," Ashley answered warmly as she paused to open her car door. "They – well – oh, dear. This is getting to be such a long tale. What I really wanted to ask you when I stopped by was whether you can come to supper tomorrow evening at our place."

"Supper?"

"Yes. Matt thought –" Ashley chatted nervously now. "Well, really I thought it would be nice to have you come over and explain everything with Matt and me and your mom and dad. That way you can tell it once and we can all move forward."

"Tell ..."

"Tomorrow evening," Ashley repeated. "Come over for supper and we'll get everything cleared up." With another quick hug Ashley assured Chrissi that the situation would turn out fine and ... well, Chrissi kind of quit hearing the words. They waved to each other as Ashley backed the car into the street.

Scores of visitors had been stopping by the hospital since Mrs. Holmes suffered her attack, and Tyler was among those who were there daily. She hadn't been conscious and strong enough to see anyone until Tuesday, and then she had refused to speak with anyone other than Tyler.

Several attempts to communicate with her had failed. Frail as she was, Mrs. Holmes would stare at the person asking her and reply with the same question regardless of what she had been asked: "Where is Tyler?" Eventually Dr. Stapp and his staff had elected to adhere to the patient's wishes. They summoned Tyler Schuster, who was listed as a family member on Mrs. Holmes' paperwork, although everyone in the county knew she had no relatives.

Tyler dreaded seeing Mrs. Holmes laid up in the hospital. He had gone to the facility when he had been called to do so the day she had been admitted. He had only glimpsed her through the ICU glass that day, and then been ushered past to complete a variety of paperwork.

He hadn't understood why he was the person she had designated to take care of such things, but he intended to find out when she awoke. Tyler had been back to the hospital several times since, either on his free time or when he was working shifts on the ambulance and they would bring a patient into the facility. She'd remained unconscious.

And so it had been days since their discussion in Mrs. Holmes' kitchen. Days since Tyler had realized that Mrs. Holmes knew the secret of his adoption. Days in which Chrissi's problems had grown in Tyler's mind to be more important than his own. They were days in which Tyler felt he had grown, somehow. He still wanted to know why Mrs. Holmes was aware of the adoption, but his feelings of betrayal had somehow diminished. Perhaps the idea that the people Tyler loved were human, and mortal, and they wouldn't be around forever – maybe forgiving and moving on were the best steps he could take.

But none of that was churning through Tyler's mind on a conscious level as he rode the elevator to the floor where Mrs. Holmes' hospital room was located. His mind was on Chrissi. He'd talked with her over the phone a couple of times each day, because somehow, texting wasn't enough and messaging wasn't enough. He needed to hear her voice, and when he did, the strain and fatigue he heard there worried him.

He tried to shake off his concerns about Chrissi as he approached the door to Mrs. Holmes' room. Pulling up a warm smile, he entered the room and moved near the bed where she reclined before speaking to her. "Well, aren't you looking good today?" he asked kindly to draw her attention.

Mrs. Holmes' eyes opened slowly, as if she had been drifting between sleep and wakefulness. Her gaze sharpened as she recognized the young man approaching her bed. "Oh, Tyler!" she exclaimed as she extended a slightly shaking hand toward him. "You came," she sighed.

"Of course I came," Tyler crooned in response. "How could I stay away when my best girl needs me?" He let her clasp his hand in hers and leaned forward to lightly kiss her forehead.

"You're a shameless flirt!" she sighed before a shadow of sadness moved across her features. "You were angry ..."

"Never," he countered as he pulled a chair near the bed. "I could never be angry with you."

"Baloney! You were upset," she argued. She closed her eyes, exhausted by the strain of conversing. "You had a right to be ..."

Tyler stayed in the room as she slept briefly. He waited and wondered and read from the Bible in the room. Presently Mrs. Holmes' pale silvery gray eyes opened slowly. And she smiled when she recognized Tyler sitting nearby.

"We should have told you," she whispered.

"It's okay," Tyler countered as he returned to the chair near the bed again.

"No, it was wrong."

Tyler couldn't maintain any irritation toward the woman he had viewed as a surrogate grandmother for so long. "It doesn't matter," he replied. "It doesn't change anything."

"But it does," she said sleepily.

Tyler didn't want to cause any stress to Mrs. Holmes, but his curiosity had been piqued. "How did you know about the adoption?" he asked carefully.

"Know about it? It was my idea," she answered as her eyes drifted closed again.

Shock rippled through Tyler. So, she had been there from the beginning. If the adoption had been her idea ... Tyler's voice nearly failed him as he whispered, "Impossible ... You're my ... what?"

"I loved you enough to place you in a home where you could have a normal life," she replied, appearing to have rallied.

Struggling with a confusing image of what might have happened, and quickly calculating ages, Tyler was dumbfounded. "You can't be my -"

"Grandmother, boy," Mrs. Holmes cut in with a hoarse laugh. "You're my grandson. And I'm proud of you."

Tears stained Tyler's cheeks as he repeated in awe, "Grandmother? How?

Her energy was quickly waning. "Go to Ashley. She has a book," Mrs. Holmes replied slowly.

"Ashley? Matt's Ashley?" Tyler asked, wondering if the woman was making any real sense. "What's she got to do with it?"

"She wrote it down. Tell her to give it to you," she said. "I'm too tired."

"Fine," he answered as he tried to find a way to give the woman a hug. "I'll go to Ashley." He pulled back to look into

Mrs. Holmes' eyes. "When I was younger, I used to wish you were my grandma," he choked. "I've loved you for so long."

CHAPTER NINE

"Dad?" Tyler spoke into his cell phone as he pulled out of the parking lot at the hospital. Without pausing to allow for a response, he continued quickly, "Mrs. Holmes is awake ... she told me I'm her grandson. She told me to go to Ashley to get a book." He stopped at a red light and waited. "Do you know anything about a book? Do you know what she's talking about?"

Jeff denied any knowledge of a book, but expressed relief that Mrs. Holmes was awake, and that she had told Tyler as much as she had. "It was out of respect and deference to her that I kept the secret," he said roughly. "She had been adamant at the time of the adoption, and I never challenged her on it later," he explained. "Now that she's told you that much, there's more I can fill in when you get home. But not much more."

Tyler didn't respond as he sped toward the home of Matt and Ashley. "I'll talk to you later," Tyler finally said.

"You will come home?"

"Yeah," he answered. "I need to get this book from Ashley, then I'll be home."

Miller's Bend was a small town and it didn't take long to drive to Matt and Ashley's home. Although the house was small, it had two main-floor bedrooms and a refinished basement where Ashley had set up a home office. Tyler had visited the house and its inhabitants thousands of times in his youth, and several times since his best friend had married.

Chrissi's car was parked in the driveway, with Melanie's behind it, Tyler noted as he parked his pickup on the street. He had kind of hoped to visit with Ashley and Matt, to learn what Ashley knew and to see if Matt could help him understand. But if they were having a family get together, Tyler wouldn't want to intrude. He'd simply ask for the book and head out.

He rapped on the door, before pushing the button for the doorbell. When the door was pulled open partially, it was Ashley who appeared in the space. Her skin was pale and worry etched her features. "Hey, Tyler," she said in welcome, but she didn't pull the door wide open.

"Hey," he responded. After a beat, he asked, "Can I come in?"

He could hear raised voices coming from another room, and knowing the layout of the house and the family members, he guessed they were at the dining table. His heart rate kicked up as he noted the increasing pitch in Chrissi's voice interspersed with rapid fire comments from the others. Ashley swung a glance that direction and then back to Tyler. "It's really not a good time," she replied. "I hate to ask, but could you come back tomorrow? We've got …" She glanced away again before concluding, "It's sort of a family situation right now."

"I've got sort of a family situation myself," Tyler countered. "I've just come from Mrs. Holmes' hospital room and she sent me here to get a book from you." He hoped to heaven Ashley knew what book he was after because Mrs. Holmes hadn't given him much to go on. And as the words rolled off his tongue, he saw the impact on Ashley. She paled further and looked chagrined as she stepped back, opening the door wider.

"She told you?" Ashley queried. And then as Tyler nodded, her expression relaxed, "Thank goodness! I hated being the only one to know her stories. Come in."

Tyler's confusion was growing along with his concern for Chrissi. Now inside the house, trailing Ashley as she moved toward the steps to the basement, he could hear more of the discussion which seemed to be intensifying by the moment. "I'll get the book," she called as she began down the steps. "Wait there."

Chrissi was crying. Tyler could hear the tremor in her voice and pinched quality as she countered a volley of questions and angry accusations. Why would her family be treating her this way? When Tyler stepped closer to the dining room, he could see that Matt was standing, pacing, and obviously very upset, while Chrissi was seated, with their mother hovering near and Byron was moving to intercept Matt as he paced.

The words became clear as Matt glared at his sister. "What were you thinking? How could you be so reckless?"

"Now Matt," Byron interjected. "She's an adult and she's a smart girl."

"Not smart enough!" Matt spat. And then focusing on Chrissi again, he accused, "You were supposed to go to college, get your degree, be a neonatal nurse. You had a dream and you've thrown it away!"

"She can still do those things -" Melanie began. "Just back off, Matthew. I'm sure Chrissi has thought this all through. It'll be fine."

Tyler couldn't believe the scene. He remembered his father telling him that Dunn had informed the gathering at Wheelers that Chrissi wasn't available, but he couldn't understand why Matt was so upset about that. Unless ... Maybe Tyler's suspicions were right and –

Chrissi was on her feet, too, now as she addressed Matt. "Ashley told me you knew. She told me you had been upset, but you accepted my secret after you had time to think about it. Why are you so mad now?" she cried.

"Knew your secret? We thought you had a boyfriend," he replied hotly. "Now you tell us you're pregnant?! That's too much, Chrissi!" He forced a hand through his curly blond hair as he tried to calm down. "Don't you understand? Mom and I worked and saved for years so you could go to college ... so you could chase your dreams ... we sacrificed for you. And you pop this surprise on us?"

"That's enough!" Melanie stepped forward, placing a hand on Matt's chest. "You cannot lay that on her. We all worked to survive. You got to chase your dream and she'll get hers, too. This just changes the way she'll have to go about it. This is not about you!"

Ignoring her mother's speech, Chrissi moved on the offensive. "Surprise? I thought you knew. I thought you'd seen the papers from the doctor's office," she began speaking only to be cut off again.

"What papers? You keep saying that. I haven't seen any papers and that doesn't really matter anyway," Matt countered. "What matters is who is responsible for this baby!"

Ashley returned with a package holding what appeared to be most of a ream of paper and handed it to Tyler. "I hope this helps," she said. And then glancing toward the drama unfolding near the dinner table, she added, "You'd better go."

"I'd better stay," Tyler answered as he handed the package back to Ashley. The magnitude of Matt's surprise at seeing Tyler step into the room was only rivaled by Chrissi's obvious relief. Both of which seeped away quickly.

Matt didn't let up; he turned his attention back to his little sister. "Who's responsible for the baby, Chrissi?"

Her chin notched up as she stepped closer to her brother. Tyler's heart ached for her as she spoke clearly. "I am, Matt. I am responsible for my child."

"And who's responsible for you?" he demanded.

Before Chrissi could answer, Tyler moved in and slipped an arm protectively around her shoulders, pulling her into his side and shifting her back slightly – further from Matt. Tyler's eyes locked on his friend's and he calmly said, "I am."

An ominous silence hung thick in the room for seconds, and then everyone was talking at once – clamoring in disbelief – asking questions, hurling condemnation. But the only thing Tyler heard through it all was Chrissi's whispered, "No, Ty. You can't."

"Yes, honey. I can," he confirmed as he turned her toward the door. "Get your jacket. We are leaving."

From behind, a hand grasped Tyler's shoulder and spun him around as he and Chrissi moved toward the exit. Anger, bordering on loathing simmered there in Matt's eyes, in his expression and in his bearing. "How could you?" Matt hissed. "You *were* my best friend!"

Ashley watched the scene play out in front of her eyes. Matt's agitation was palatable, and it disturbed her that the man she'd married could be so volatile and unreasonable. Chrissi had withdrawn from the discussion as soon as Tyler stepped in on her behalf. The memory of Chrissi's terror the day of the shooting came back to Ashley, along with the impression she'd had that the young woman's behavior seemed similar to women who had been victimized.

Tyler stepped toward the much taller man, forcing him to retreat a step. "I *am* your best friend. This won't be the end of it. But you have to collect yourself," he said with quiet calmness. "Your mom was right. This isn't about you – it's about Chris. How dare you make her feel like she's done something to you? How dare you try to make her feel guilty? She's your sister – you owe her your love and support."

"Seems like you've been providing that," Matt sneered.

"Matt!" Ashley stepped between them. "Tyler's right. You don't know what's going on. And you owe it to yourself to shut up and save the relationships you have with your sister, your best friend and your wife," she advised.

"My wife?" His attention was drawn to Ashley now. "What about my wife? You're siding with them?" he asked in disbelief.

"You are over-reacting -"

"Over-reacting?" he argued. "My best friend took advantage of my baby sister!"

The house door slammed behind Tyler as he and Chrissi headed for his pickup. She stopped to grab her backpack out of her car and then hit the button on the fob to lock the doors before sliding the key into her pocket. They silently strode past Melanie's car, into the street and up to the driver's side door of Tyler's pickup. He opened the door and boosted Chris up onto the seat. She pushed the backpack across the seat to the door and shifted into the center of the bench seat.

She stared straight ahead as Tyler settled behind the wheel. He started the engine and shifted the pickup into gear. But before he'd let out the clutch, her hand touched his, drawing his attention, and then pulling away. Shifting back into neutral, he focused on Chrissi. "What?" he asked, searching her features in the mottled light cast by the city fixtures.

"You can't do this – Matt will hate you," she said. "We have to go back inside."

She had spunk, he thought. That, and a ton of loyalty. "We're not going back tonight," he replied, and then paused. "Matt needs some time."

"Time isn't going to help," she countered sadly. "You made him think you've wronged me and he isn't going to forgive either of us."

Tyler touched Chrissi's chin, gently turning her face toward his own, before speaking again. "Time will help. We haven't wronged anyone and there is nothing for him to forgive."

Chrissi closed her eyes against the intensity of Tyler's gaze. She was still trembling inside from the explosive scene with her brother. And something in the way Ty touched her soul made her tremble more.

Tyler's words were comforting, but the pain from Matt's reaction was etched in her mind and on her heart. How could he have reacted so harshly? Conversely, Tyler had been completely accepting of her and of the situation. He hadn't seemed the least bit surprised when he'd stepped into that room after hearing that she was pregnant. He'd intervened, and accepted her, and moved to protect her from the verbal attack. He'd shielded her and removed her from the situation.

His hand cupped Chrissi's cheek and she was growing more attuned to his touch each time. She found herself leaning slightly into his gentle caress. "Let me take care of you," he whispered. "You'll be alright if we're together."

She didn't respond, although Chrissi's spirit soared at the idea of letting Ty tend to her. He turned his attention to driving, and left her to her thoughts. She'd known him forever and had developed a huge crush on him a couple years ago. But in recent years, as she'd matured, she'd grown to know Ty as a person and, especially recently, as a close friend. She suspected she could love him – maybe she already did – but had been afraid to let it show.

They arrived at Mrs. Holmes' Victorian house, where Chrissi lived in the basement apartment. She shivered as she gazed at the dark, intimidating structure. Normally Chrissi loved the house, but tonight …

"Hey," Ty sighed. "I just thought of something." His smile was a sad one as he added, "You should have left the keys to the car with Matt, so he can move it out of the way in the morning … or he'll have to walk to his studio."

She turned her head slightly then, just enough to see Ty's reaction, and replied coolly, "The walk may do him some good. And besides, I have a passive-aggressive streak." She finally smiled when she added, "Matt will understand."

Tyler laughed lightly and Chrissi returned her attention to the imposing house. "I suppose, I'd better go in," she suggested, but didn't move to exit the pickup.

"Come on," Tyler encouraged. "I'll go inside with you."

He helped her down from the truck, and escorted her to the door. Silently they entered, making their way down the steps and into the apartment. The house creaked in the way that older houses do sometimes, and Chrissi's breath caught. She was jumpy for no good reason, but Tyler pulled her close. "Hey?" he said softly. "You going to be alright here alone?"

She nodded a quick response and sniffled. And then the emotions rolled over her: Matt's disappointment and agitation, her parents' surprise, her own feelings of guilt and shame, and her deepening feelings for Tyler. She couldn't – no ... she shouldn't – become attached to him. She shouldn't let herself rely on him. But he'd saved her tonight, and if she was honest with herself he'd been saving her since the moment she'd returned from Chicago. She didn't know how she would get through this night alone in the massive old house. The movement of her nodding morphed into a negative head shake. Her lips quivered and a quiet sob escaped, with a nearly non-existent, "No."

Be strong and courageous. The phrase popped into Tyler's mind as he held Chrissi and waited for her to regain her composure. It was from the Bible, and if he remembered correctly, the phrase appeared in multiple passages. The Lord directs men to be strong and courageous ... to be men of courage. It might take some courage to stand by Chrissi through the coming months, he thought. It would definitely take courage to face Matt again tomorrow, but he would do it, if she wanted him to; if she was able to accept his feelings.

Chrissi's desperation began to dissolve as Ty held her and comforted her while she cried out her emotional tide. He was strong and steady, and oh, how relieved she'd been when he appeared in the doorway to Matt's dining room. She was confident that her family loved her, but she'd been so overwhelmed by their shock and Matt's anger when they learned she was pregnant, that she had faltered. She'd felt so alone as they'd bombarded her with questions. Ty's appearance had felt as if a safety net had been tightened beneath her, protecting her from a painful fall.

His confidence had strengthened Chrissi when he stepped between her and Matt, wrapping her protectively in his embrace. He hadn't hesitated and he hadn't questioned her.

Her brain began thinking again, rather than simply floating in the wonderful sensations that came with accepting the solace he offered. She raised a hand to interfere with the gentle strokes he'd been brushing down her hair. She pulled away marginally and her gaze darted to his face. Why hadn't he questioned her? Why hadn't Ty been as surprised as her family had when he'd heard that she was pregnant?

He didn't speak as he seemed to be waiting for her to say what was on her mind. She struggled for the best way to ask, and finally settled on the straight-forward approach. "You knew?" The words came quietly, almost as if she was afraid to speak them.

Remarkably Tyler understood the question. He closed his eyes for a second, as if to steel himself and then answered with a slight shrug. "I suspected," he confirmed. At her inquisitive look, he added, "Your weight loss, the vomiting, the crackers and water; the mysterious appointment out of town … and the papers in your car. It kind of added up to this."

Chrissi lowered her head and tried to turn away, but he still held her loosely. She didn't fight to be free of his hold, because she hadn't really wanted that anyway. "You must think …" she mumbled quietly, but didn't finish the thought.

Tyler touched a finger beneath her chin, tenderly lifting Chrissi's face to meet his gaze so she might truly listen and understand. "I must think you've been through something terrible. I must think you are incredibly strong and resilient," he whispered, as he urged her closer. "I must think your faith is strengthening you do deal with this."

He held her close once again, stroking her dark hair and the length of her back. Together they rocked gently from side to side as Chrissi rode the waves of conflicting emotions. Questions rising in her mind, but not finding voice until at last one broke free. "You don't think I did something?"

"I don't know what you mean?" he responded.

"That I chose this … or caused it to happen?"

"Never," he replied with vehemence. "Chris, I know you. I don't believe for a second that you had any control of the circumstances. Whatever happened, the choice had been taken away from you."

CHAPTER TEN

The change was subtle as they stood, locked together and swaying to some unheard musical rhythm. Tyler's instincts flared. He loved Chrissi. He'd denied it for more than two years. He'd told himself it wasn't possible; that it wasn't real. But it was real and even though she was younger – a lot younger – he hoped and prayed they could build a relationship together. If Chrissi felt something similar for him, they might have a chance.

He didn't think it through, but his lips slid across Chrissi's velvet-smooth cheek to find her lips. It was a light kiss that they shared. Easy and sweet, but filled with emotion. And Tyler's heart soared as Chrissi returned the gesture before she pulled away. Moisture stood in her eyes as she smiled at Tyler. Oh, how he loved this woman.

She backed away and lowered her gaze, quietly saying, "We can't have a relationship."

Stepping close, Tyler captured her hands, but didn't pull her into his arms again. He couldn't stop the smile from breaking across his face as he spoke. "We already have a relationship, Chris. We just have never defined it."

Then as she let herself be enveloped in his embrace once again, she heard his whispered words, and felt his breath as he spoke close to her ear, "I love you. I will be here with you. I will see you through this and through everything that is to come. I will take care of you. Forever."

Her body hitched with a quiet sob. With tears in her eyes and on her cheeks, she said, "You can't." She paced a few steps away to regain her ability to think clearly.

"I can if you'll let me," he began, but she cut him off.

"I can't let you," she countered. "You just feel sorry for me."

"That's the last thing I feel for you," he answered with a low chuckle. "We've been friends for a long time. I didn't even realize it was more than that until you took off to save your cousin. It was hell, not knowing where you were and if you were alright," he explained as the remembered anguish twisted Ty's features. "I was going crazy with worry, but I couldn't tell anyone, because I had no legitimate reason to be so concerned about you."

Ty paced in the tiny apartment, wishing for more space. The air in the underground chamber was old and sad, and he felt his heart race. His breaths were shallow as he continued to reveal his own secrets. "I must not have been too discreet though, because Dad figured it out. Once they'd talked with Byron, and had an idea where you were headed, he shared as much information as he could with me," he continued to speak as he paced. Suddenly, Ty stopped right in front of Chrissi; he faced her and lowered his eyes. "I know more than you realize," he confessed. "And what I don't know for sure, I've pieced together."

Chrissi's heart rate ratcheted up and her hopes took wing. Tyler knew the truth and he wasn't repulsed; he didn't judge her, and he loved her. And then her outlook plummeted as she felt the bile rise: Tyler knew; and his father knew, and probably the sheriff ... who else? She'd thought that, at least locally, she alone had knowledge of the circumstances of her captivity while in Chicago. She'd thought she could bury the truth in layers of denial and save face somehow. But now, what would she do? The story would be out. It would be fodder for the gossips. She dashed to the sink where she lost the meager supper she'd eaten.

A strong masculine hand rubbed gentle circles on her back, even as she wished to be alone. Why was he so caring? Why was he able to give so much support and understanding? Why did Tyler keep coming to her aid, when logic should have had him running for the proverbial hills?

She began shivering, which advanced quickly to shaking. Tyler noted Chrissi's rapid, shallow breathing and moved her to the couch where he had her sit with her head lowered between her knees. He lovingly covered her with an afghan from the back of the couch to keep her from getting chilled. The whole time he talked to her in low, soothing tones, trying to calm her jangled nerves. She was exhibiting early signs of shock, and he didn't want the condition to explode. He continued trying to pacify and console her until he sensed that her breathing was returning to normal.

She straightened, and pulled the afghan tightly around her shoulders as she leaned back. With her eyes closed, she let her head fall against the wall behind the couch. "So everybody knows everything?" she whispered harshly. "Every nasty detail?"

"No," Tyler denied. "You are the only one who knows everything. I am the only one who knows what the local cops know about the time you were held captive and that you are now pregnant. Everyone else knows only one part or the other."

Things were mixing around in Chrissi's mind: everybody knew, nobody knew. "What are you saying?" she asked tiredly. And then her eyes flew open as another thought caught Chrissi. "My family knows," she countered.

"They'd rather believe that you and I … well," he paused, as he admitted to himself how much he'd prefer that be the truth as well. "They'd rather believe we've been together, than to consider what might have happened in Chicago."

"So you're saying … what, exactly?" Her voice was weary.

"This baby is ours," he replied with conviction deepening the timbre of his voice.

She sat up straighter and speared Tyler with an accusing glare. "And just how did that happen?"

"We …" he cast about for a plausible explanation, before continuing. "We'd been secretly seeing each other and … we got engaged at Christmastime?" We winced when he heard the words – that wouldn't work. "There was a New Year's Eve party and we got carried away …" That sounded torrid. "After the trauma of my dad being shot, I was distraught and you comforted me?" In his dreams.

Chris was looking at Ty as though he'd grown horns, when the next wave of nausea hit. She didn't actually vomit this time, but she needed to settle her stomach. Ty, having been through this with her before, retrieved the package of crackers from the counter and a glass of water. "Do you get sick this much every day, or is it the stress this time?" he asked gently.

After downing a couple of crackers, and delicately sipping the tepid water, she looked at him and smiled. "I think it's the stress," she replied. "I don't want to lie to my family and I don't want to ask my friends to lie for me."

Ty's impression of Chrissi grew immensely. A lie would help protect her from the gossip, and he'd have gladly had a role in it. But her morals wouldn't allow for that. "I'd do it for you," he said.

"You can't, Ty," she replied. "I won't let you. You'd be a hypocrite and I won't be a part of making you into something you don't want to be." She reached out slowly, hesitantly, and brushed her fingers lightly against his rough jaw.

He caught her hand, and turned to gently kiss it, before nestling it into his own. His gaze captured hers and he repeated, "I'd do anything to protect you."

"Not that. We can't build a life on lies," she said. "Look at the emotional damage caused by the secret of your own adoption. We can't do that to my baby. And I doubt you could live with yourself – at least not happily – knowing that you were deceiving the people you love."

She had him on that point, he conceded as he waited for inspiration. The only inspiration that he felt was the need to be with her, to love her and protect her, to grow old together and live out their lives together. "Alright," he sighed. "We don't build an alternate truth. But you'll let me be your partner? You'll marry me?"

She'd been on such a cycle of extreme emotions that Chrissi didn't know what other argument to press in opposition. She really had wanted that – to be loved by Tyler – but had buried that wish. And now here it was laid out as a question for her. Her future was in her hands ... and in the seconds while she considered the options, he reassured her with hushed sincerity.

"I've liked you from the start, Chris. I've respected and admired who you've grown to be and I truly, deeply love you," he said as the emotions reflected in his eyes reinforced the words. "But I want to be clear on this. You need to understand my intentions." He leaned close to her and a rich sensation developed in her chest, as she held her breath waiting for the rest of his proclamation to be revealed. "This isn't a noble gesture. I'm not asking you to marry me to save your honor. It's more selfish than that – yes, I want to love you, honor you and cherish you; but I want that and more from you in return. I want to be the person you share your life with – the highs and the lows. Your joys and fears will be mine; and mine will be yours."

Such beautiful words; such wonderful sentiment. But there was one more consideration. "And my baby?" she asked as tears coursed down her cheeks.

"I will love him or her as my own. I will be the father to all your children," he answered. Remembering Jeff's words the night Tyler had raised the question of his own paternity. "A wise man recently told me that fatherhood has much more to do with love than it has to do with biology."

She sniffled and stood, as she wiped the tears away and tried, once again to regain her composure. She had expected Ty to stand as well, but instead he slipped from the couch to kneel on the floor, as he pulled something from his pocket. Opening a vintage jeweler's box, he carefully took a tastefully styled diamond ring from within. His gaze raised to meet Chrissi's as he asked again, "Will you marry me?"

She swallowed her fears and embraced her hopes as she nodded. "Yes, Ty. I will."

He surged to his feet, and then hugging her again, he whispered, "Thank God. I love you, Chris. I'll prove it to you – you'll see."

"I know," she replied. "And, Ty?" She pulled away a bit, so he could see her expression as she said the words. "I love you, too."

A half hour or so later they approached the kitchen door of Jeff Schuster's home, and once again Chrissi balked. "Maybe I should have stayed at my apartment," she suggested timidly. Tyler wrapped an arm across her shoulders and unhurriedly encouraged her forward in stride with him. She sighed and looked into his face, "I mean. I'd be okay there. I was just a little shaken," she concluded. "I could go back."

Tyler's grip on her shoulder tightened as he kept walking. "I'm not leaving you there alone," he said quietly. "So either you stay at your mom's or Matt's or here," he offered as options. "I'm not trying to order you around. It's just been a rough evening for you and I'd feel better if you aren't alone. I think you'd feel better, too."

"Just for tonight," she conceded as they reached the entrance. "I'll stay with Mom until Mrs. Holmes is released. Then I can go back to the apartment."

"If that's what you want," he confirmed. "Otherwise you're welcome here. You can have the guest room. It's private and right next to the bathroom."

The porch light cast a warm glow that surrounded the couple as Chrissi's questioning gaze darted to Tyler's face; rosiness spread through her cheeks, as he waited for her to speak. In her bashfulness, she managed to ask, "What about you? Where will you be?"

"No worries," he acknowledged her concerns with a wry grin. "I'll be on duty. I'm scheduled to work tonight."

"Oh."

Was that disappointment?

He laughed as he pulled her close. "Dad would horsewhip me if I infringed on you." And then, growing serious, he lovingly cupped her face. "I will never knowingly or intentionally do anything that will hurt you." Slowly, he lowered his lips to hers and accentuated his words with an easy, light kiss. When he began to retreat, Chrissi hesitantly trailed her fingers through his dark, wavy hair to touch his nape and stop him from pulling away. And then she kissed him.

Although the kiss seemed tentative and shy, the knowledge that Chrissi was willing to show her feelings through a physical outlet was a relief. He knew they would have to take things slowly and carefully, but this was a good start.

Once inside the house, Tyler yelled to his father, letting him know he had arrived. He and Chrissi hung their jackets on the pegs near the door. "Did you get that book?" Jeff called out in response. With fingers entwined, Tyler led her into the living room.

"No, I forgot about the book, but I've brought something much better," he said. When Jeff looked up from the magazine he'd been reading, his expression lit with happiness. The goofy grin his son bore and the shy smile that graced Chrissi's cheeks, made him hope there had been a breakthrough. Jeff's focus dropped to the kids' hands which were tightly clasping each other.

Rising from his comfortable chair, Jeff paused. "Hi Chrissi," he said in welcome.

He glanced at his son, who seemed to have lost the ability to speak, and then back at Chrissi, who had drawn back slightly, to try to hide behind Ty's arm. She was still clinging to him though, and Jeff took that as a good sign. "You kids eat yet?"

he asked casually, as he stepped past them into the kitchen. "I was just gonna warm up some more casserole."

"We could eat," Tyler allowed. He hadn't expected to feel nervous about telling his father their news, but suddenly he was. They followed Jeff back into the room they had just passed through and Tyler cleared his throat. "Dad."

Jeff pulled a casserole from the refrigerator, glanced at the pair, before continuing toward the microwave. He placed the dish inside and pushed the button for the rewarm setting. He regarded the couple as he waited for the update from his son. "Out with it then," he ordered kindly.

Chrissi had expected a slightly resigned announcement that they'd be "gettin' hitched – soon", but to her surprise that wasn't at all the way Tyler presented the situation to his father. He gazed tenderly into her eyes for a moment, and then beaming with pride and joy, Ty turned his attention to Jeff and said, "The good Lord has blessed me with the woman of my dreams, Dad. Chrissi and I are going to get married."

Chrissi's relief was tremendous as she realized she'd been waiting for Jeff's response to be negative, but it wasn't. His smile broadened and he threw his arms open wide to engulf his son in a bear hug. "Congratulations! You are one lucky son of a buck!" he exclaimed. Tyler let loose of Chrissi's hand to return the hug as his father thumped him on the back. "Your mother would be so happy for you."

"Thanks, Dad," Tyler responded. His voice sounded choked as he looked to Chrissi. "I just can't believe you are really willing to have me," he said humbly.

"No, Ty. I am the lucky one here," she said with quiet reverence. "I won't let you down."

"Now don't go taking that attitude with him, missy," Jeff advised as he stepped closer to her. "He's the lucky one, and you'd best keep reminding him of the fact," he added with a wink. He raised his arms in invitation for a hug, and Chrissi hesitated. A shadow flickered across Jeff's features, as if he suddenly remembered the reason for her reserve. "It's okay. We'll get there," he said philosophically. Then he clasped her hand in a quick shake and said, "Welcome to the family."

Chrissi wondered how welcome she'd be when Jeff learned the rest of the story, but the conversation didn't immediately go there. The trio enjoyed a quick supper and the men talked about all sorts of things that weren't important. They bantered about the recently concluded March Madness basketball tournaments, the price of gas, the fact that the spring fishing opener was only a couple weekends away and who would clear the table.

Eventually, Jeff asked again about the book and it piqued Chrissi's attention. He'd referenced it when she and Ty had first arrived, and she wondered about it now. "What book?" she interjected.

Tyler apologized and then explained that he'd been summoned to Mrs. Holmes' hospital room on her edict earlier that day. "She is my grandmother," he said solemnly to his fiancée. "Remember when she had the attack, I told you that she knew about my adoption?" Chris nodded numbly. "Today she told me she's my grandmother. She was too weak to tell me much. But she said she loves me and she's proud of the man I am …"

Chrissi touched his hand lightly. "She and I have a lot in common," she commented. "But how's she your grandmother? I thought she and Harold never had any children?"

"I don't know," Tyler confessed. "She was too weak to explain. She sent me to Ashley to get a book. I don't know any more than that," he added sadly.

"That's why you were at the house tonight?" she asked in astonishment. "For this mysterious book?"

He nodded. "It was a good thing I was there, too," he said, wincing away from the memory of Matt's accusations against Chrissi.

Jeff's curiosity flared as he looked between the two. "What happened?"

Tyler looked to his beloved, and his brow creased. "I'm not really sure how it started, but it blew up fast. What did happen?" he directed toward Chrissi.

She squirmed in her seat, not really wanting to recount the conversation. She looked at the men who were watching her curiously. One's gaze radiated love and acceptance; the other shown with deep concern, but also acceptance, and love of a different sort – a Christian love. "It's okay, Chrissi-girl," Jeff said. "You don't have to explain anything."

Tears welled and her sinuses burned. It was true. Perhaps because she didn't feel compelled to explain, the words poured out. She told them that Ashley had invited her to supper with her and Matt, and her parents. She'd been told that that they knew her secret and accepted it. She explained that she'd figured Matt had known because of the papers she'd left in the car, but he'd been totally dumbfounded when she'd mentioned the baby.

Chrissi paused, waiting for a reaction from Tyler's dad, but there was none. "I'm so confused," she confided. "It just doesn't make sense … Ashley said he knew."

"Chris," Ty drew her attention. "Matt never saw those papers."

"What?!"

"I saw them ... the morning we pulled your car out of the ditch. I was the first one there. I unlocked the car and started it, and I saw them on the floor under the edge of the seat. I picked them up and noticed ..." he glanced at his father, but quickly returned his attention to Chrissi. "I wasn't sure what it meant, but I didn't think you'd want Matt or Riley seeing them, so I put them in my pocket."

"I put them back in your car when I started it for you before you left Wheelers' on Sunday afternoon," he confessed. "I should have talked to you, but it took me a while to digest. And in the meantime, my questions became irrelevant."

"Matt never saw them?" she asked dumbly. "Then what was Ashley talking about? Why would she have said they all knew my secret?"

"I think I can help with that question," Jeff interjected. "Sunday ... at the Wheelers' ... after you left, Shelby was trying to get Dunn interested in you."

"Matchmaking," Tyler interpreted.

"And Dunn pointed out that you were 'unavailable'," Jeff concluded. "Matt was mighty shocked at that. So I decided it was time to go and hurried Dunn out of there before he blew it for you kids."

"We're not kids, Dad," Ty pointed out.

"Ya' are to me."

There was a conversational vacuum. The clock ticked. The refrigerator hummed. And then Chrissi gasped. "I must have nearly given Matt a coronary tonight," she said sadly. "No wonder he reacted so ..."

"Badly," Tyler finished for her. "Irrationally. Like a flippin' maniac." He touched her chin and she faced him with regret written in her eyes. "You can't take responsibility for his actions, Chris. You can't. He's a big boy and he's responsible for his own outbursts."

She slid the chair back and began to rise. "I have to call him and apologize. I've disappointed him so much."

"No, you don't," Tyler's voice was harsh, freezing her in a half-stand. "He needs to apologize to you; not the other way around."

Sadness moved across her features as she dropped back into the chair. "I hope I haven't destroyed your friendship," she said softly to Tyler. "You shouldn't have told him you were responsible for me and the baby."

"Hold on," Jeff commanded. "Now you've lost me." Turning a questioning eye on his son, he asked with a note of censure, "You're responsible?"

Tyler straightened in his chair, meeting his father's impervious glare. "From this day forward, yes, I am responsible."

Understanding passed between the men, and then Jeff turned again to Chrissi. With the utmost kindness, he offered his assurance, "We three are the only souls in Miller's Bend who know any of the details of your captivity, unless you've shared it with your family. And we can keep it that way, if that's what you want."

"The other officers? Don't they know?" she asked timidly.

Jeff explained that the paperwork revolving around her case did not reflect the details, however, he said, Agent Stockard had shared his suspicions that Chrissi had been drugged and violated during her captivity. "He wanted me to keep an extra eye out for your welfare," he concluded. "Nice man."

Chrissi teared up again as she remembered the federal agent who had befriended her and saved her life. "He died trying to protect me," she said with quiet reverence. Stockard had taken multiple bullets the day of the shooting in an attempt to shield Chrissi. His protective vest would have kept him safe, but one bullet had clipped an artery in his neck. He'd died at the scene.

Someday she would share with Tyler, and maybe Jeff, the way the undercover agent had helped strengthen her while she was held captive in Chicago. He had sneaked a tiny Bible to her and befriended her as much as possible, tried to protect her from the guard who had drugged and abused her, and how he had brought her a protective Kevlar blanket just minutes before the house swarmed with federal agents and gunfire had erupted.

He had given the other agents her location and information proving she was a victim, not a perp, so that she wouldn't be humiliated by being processed with the criminals. He'd even escorted her back to her home town days later, meeting with the local law enforcement officials to assure her continued safety. Except the criminal – the one who had drugged her and abused her – had followed them. He'd burst into the police station interrogation room and opened fire, killing Stockard and wounding Police Chief Jeff Schuster, before being taken down by Officer Pendleton.

She shivered at the memory, but didn't panic. Tyler was there, instantly holding her in his strong arms, supporting her with his love and faith. "You okay?" he asked, his voice cracking slightly.

"I'm exhausted," she confessed.

"I'll get your things from the truck," Ty said as he eased away from her.

Jeff cleared his throat, and shot his son another questioning look.

"Chrissi's shaken up. I told her she could stay in the guest room here," he replied. "I'll take the couch until I go to work. Unless you think it would be better if I went to my own apartment?" he said, intentionally deferring to his father's wishes and advice.

The older man considered the circumstances only a moment before he nodded his acceptance. "It should be fine," he said.

CHAPTER ELEVEN

Ashley was not having a good morning. The newspapers had gone out in the mail and onto the newsstands overnight. The phone had been ringing non-stop since she'd opened up at 7:45 a.m. Shelby had written a story about a proposed expansion of the local cheese plant and people were excited. The story was well composed, and Ashley had been confident that the move would be seen as a great advancement for the community; however it seemed there were citizens opposed to allowing one company to "take over the town" as it had been put to her several times already.

Of course, in all fairness, she had also taken numerous calls from people who believed that the expansion would be fantastic, adding to the city coffers through increased sales tax, and helping all the local businesses by doubling the number of employees, and thus payroll, when the expansion was complete.

On top of the fact that the Chronicle was receiving a flood of phone calls, Bobbie, the receptionist hadn't shown up for work that day. She hadn't called either. Ashley had called Shelby to come in to help field calls.

Ashley, with her elbows propped on her desk, stared blankly at the monitor in front of her, when Shelby arrived. "Hey, Ash!"

she called cheerfully from the front office as she rounded the counter. "Never fear, reinforcements have arrived!" She strode to the back office and asked more seriously, "What can I do to help? I just can't believe Bobbie would blow off work without even having the courtesy to call."

Ashley shrugged. Bobbie's behavior had grown erratic and Ashley wasn't nearly as surprised as she might have been about the unexplained absence. However, she knew the sheriff had been back to talk with Bobbie and her son, Adam, about the break-in at the newspaper the week before. She didn't know the outcome, but expected to hear from Sheriff Dunn soon.

Shelby sensed that her best friend had deeper worries than an absent employee. "Hey? What's wrong?" she queried as she took in Ashley's pale skin tone, puffy eyes and the dark circles below them.

Tears brimmed in her blue eyes, but Ashley blinked them back. "I can't talk about it now," she said, sitting taller in her chair. "If I do, I'll cry. I'll explain after work, if you have time," she sighed.

"I'll make time," Shelby asserted before the phone started ringing again.

It was a frantic day, and after an angry call from a low-level manager at the cheese plant, Ashley decided she should have some legal advice before things got out of hand. She called Mason Alexander, a young lawyer with political aspirations and a friend of her husband's, and arranged for him to meet with her and Shelby that afternoon.

Mason arrived, just as the phones quieted and the three were able to have a productive meeting. He reviewed Shelby's notes and tape recording of the interview from which she'd written the story and confidently assured the two women that neither they, nor the newspaper could have any liability if, as the manager indicated, he wanted to sue. "You've done everything right," he said. "Just be sure you keep your records in a safe place so you have them if he follows through on his threats."

Ashley was relieved to have the advice of a professional in law and thanked him. The two women also congratulated Mason on his recent appointment the State's Attorney office in the county. "I have every confidence that you will be a great replacement for old Mr. Parrsons," Shelby concluded as she left the back office to wait on the customer who had appeared up front.

Ashley inquired as to whether Mason had decided to run for the state legislature and was rewarded with a smile and a nod. "Sure have," he confirmed. "I can do that for one session, and then make a run for Governor. The first pass will be to get name recognition; maybe by the next election I will actually have a shot at winning."

She wished him well in his plans and thanked Mason again for the consultation, expecting him to head back to his office – or wherever he was going next. However, Mason looked as if he had more on his mind; opened his mouth as if to speak and then closed it without a sound.

"What?" Ashley demanded. When he didn't respond, she stood, fighting down the instinct to demand to know what the man was thinking. "Look. It's been a rough day," she said. "If you have something else to add, please just say it."

Mason glanced to the front lobby, where Shelby was still occupied with customers, and then met Ashley's gaze. "Matt stopped by …"

She stiffened. "I don't think -"

Mason raised a hand, asking her to wait. "I'm not getting in the middle of it – I promise. I just thought you should know he's very upset," he explained.

"Good. He should be," she said quickly and then immediately regretted the shrewish outburst. She softened her stance and her voice. "I know you're good friends, but he was way out of line last night," she explained, without really explaining. "I was shocked that he could be so crass and judgmental."

"He didn't tell me the specifics," Mason said quietly. "And I don't need to know. But I am absolutely sure that he's sorry. He doesn't know what to do to make it up to you -"

"Me?" Ashley cut in. Fire danced in her eyes as she explained, "I wasn't a victim in this. His sister was; and his friend was. They are the ones he needs to make amends with."

"He's worried about you," Mason said with heartfelt concern. "He's desperately afraid of losing you because of whatever happened last night."

The despised tears stood in her eyes once again as she faced her husband's friend. "He should be." Mason, having listened to Matt's ravings earlier, and Ashley's comments now, was certain that the two could forgive each other if they would just get together and talk it out. They were both miserable, and as he watched, the tears spilled over onto Ashley's cheeks.

He thought of his sister, Katie, and the way she would cry when she was frustrated or scared or overwhelmed, or for any other variety of reasons. He thought of Katie and the way she would sometimes continue to cry until he or their parents would offer some comfort. And with that thought, he set his briefcase aside and pulled her into a quick hug. "Matt loves you," he said. "You have to know that's the most important thing."

Of course, love without understanding can be a very volatile force. And Matt, who had entered through the Chronicle's back entrance, could have waited a minute and asked for an explanation. But instead, when he saw his wife, being held by his friend, he panicked. Assuming the worst, he fled, slamming the door closed in his wake.

Ashley jerked away from Mason. Her heart jammed in her throat she dashed for the exit, yanking the 120-year-old door open and barreling outdoors. "Matt!" she called as she spotted him leaping into his classic Camaro. He didn't look her way as he hit the gas and sped past her. Ashley cringed as she watched him blow through a stop sign and across Main Street, narrowly avoiding a collision with an older-style Buick.

Mason was beside her then, on the sidewalk. He mumbled an oath as he watched the Camaro speeding out of sight. "Just when I thought it couldn't get worse," Ashley muttered. "How am I going to get him to listen to me now?"

"I'll catch up with him," Mason offered. "Clear things up – at least where you and I are concerned."

Matt's heart pounded hard as if he'd run a half-marathon. Only, he hadn't. He'd driven a couple of blocks, nearly killed old Mrs. Fields in her 1976 Buick, and probably destroyed his image in Ashley's eyes. As if his actions last night hadn't already done that. Matt pulled into the parking lot behind a storage building on a back street; shifted the car into Park and cut the engine. His hands were shaking and his vision blurred.

Feeling as if he couldn't draw another breath, he leaned his head back against the seat and tried to focus his mind by just breathing. *Breathe in. Breathe out. Breathe in. Breathe out.*

Ashley despises me. No, she doesn't. Breathe in. Breathe out. Breathe in. Breathe out.

The memories of last night's supper with his family seeped into his mind. That's when the trouble started. Chrissi had been nervous and fidgety, so he'd figured it was best to get the issue out of the way. He'd told her that they all knew her secret so she could relax.

Subconsciously, he snorted. They hadn't known her secret at all. He'd thought it was a big deal when Erik had implied that Chrissi was seeing someone; the bombshell she'd casually dropped last night blew that one out of the water. Pregnant. By Tyler. The successive thoughts hit him again like the one-two punch of heavyweight boxer. The words were repulsive to him.

He strung together a sequence of words he rarely used. He didn't dare talk to Tyler yet, or they'd end up in a fight.

Matt attempted to scour the stinging sensation from his eyes. He thought of the evening before. He'd been surprised to see his friend appear in the doorway from the kitchen, alright. But he'd been on the wings of a righteous rave, and was so comfortable with Tyler after all their years of friendship, that he had not let his presence influence the tirade.

Looking back he was feeling ashamed of his behavior. His actions had made him into the bad guy. And Tyler, if one could judge by Chrissi's expression in that moment, had become her knight in shining armor, as he'd stepped in and shielded her from Matt's verbal assault. Matt winced at the memory. Maybe … he'd been harsh toward Chrissi. And toward Tyler. Ashley had certainly jumped to their defense.

Okay, he admitted, only to himself … he had definitely been too harsh. And quick to judge. Maybe he had overreacted.

Just as Ashley had said when she intervened between himself and Tyler. The urge to go after Tyler reared up again. He wouldn't do that though – not today. Somehow he figured, even though going toe to toe with his former best friend would relieve his own frustrations, the act would end up alienating the women he loved. No, he thought, Chrissi, their mom and Ashley would never speak to him again.

Ashley. He squeezed his eyes more tightly closed as a new torment sliced into his consciousness. The image of his wife in Mason's arms stung his pride. One little argument and she was clinging to another man. And then he heard her voice, repeating the words she'd said last night. The words that had begun their fight, "You're over-reacting." It seemed as if she was saying the words again and again. She hadn't stood up for him; she'd backed the opposition. Wasn't a wife supposed to support her man?

His body lurched when something banged against his car. Jerking his eyes open Matt realized Ashley stood outside his driver door – talking a mile a minute. Against his will, he smiled slightly, thinking that she could go on for hours if nothing interrupted her. Her cheeks were flushed and her red hair danced and swirled around her face as if commanded by a tempest. And her eyes sparked as she paused for a breath and then began a new onslaught. Again he heard the phrase, "You're over-reacting."

She was making hand gestures that seemed to imply that Matt should join her outside the car. He smiled more broadly. Ashley had come after him, and that was a good sign. He opened the door and stepped out, thinking he'd let her wear herself down a bit before getting too close, but she immediately launched herself into his arms. The impact forced him back against the car and he took advantage of holding her close. He'd captured her and could feel the energy coursing through her body. She was in high dungeon and continued to relate to him – in too many words – that he was a fool if he believed there was anything between her and Mason.

The sparks in her eyes had been fueled by righteous anger moments ago and that passion remained but it had begun to transform. Matt's senses read the change before his mind caught up - before he remembered his hurt and his own disappointments and anger. Suddenly, he took charge, spinning his wife so Ashley's back was against the car, and his lanky body shielded her from view, should anyone pass this way. His lips touched hers as she continued to sputter about his apparent insanity. "I'm a fool," he whispered. Again they touched, and her speech faltered.

His hands slid to her face, where his thumbs gently wiped her angry tears away. Their gazes caught and held; and their breathing, labored seconds earlier, suspended. His focus dropped to her lips. "I'm a fool," he repeated. And then Matt slowly lowered his head and gently kissed her. She sighed, and leaned into the kiss, into him, returning to him, accepting him.

When they ended the kiss, she whispered, "You still over-reacted."

"I'm beginning to see that," he replied.

She cocked an eyebrow and he read cautious curiosity in her expression before she spoke. "You're conceding?"

"Not entirely," he countered. "But I'm willing to enter into negotiations." He smiled as she pulled him close again and pushed up on her tip-toes to lightly kiss his cheek.

"I'm glad you are a man who can be reasoned with," she offered with a touch of sass in her voice. Then she sobered and stepped to the side, out of his embrace. The serious way she looked at him made Matt's breath catch. "You scared me last night," she said quietly. "I couldn't believe the way you were behaving. And then you left."

"I walked to my studio. Spent the night there," he intoned, as he remembered the way his temper had spiked at discovering Chrissi's car sitting behind his closed garage door, locking his own vehicle inside. "She left her car, you know. She went home with Ty."

"Jeff brought her by early this morning to get it, so she could drive herself to school," Ashley confirmed. She paused, debating whether to push the topic, and then forged ahead. "He wanted to tell you that she'd stayed in the guest room at his house; she didn't go home with Tyler."

Some of the tension in Matt's features ebbed at hearing her words, and Ashley hoped the knowledge would ease some of the feelings her husband had been harboring. "He also wanted you to know that Tyler had the midnight shift on the ambulance last night," she added. Without elaborating, she knew Matt understood the implication: the two most definitely did not spend the night together.

An annoying embryonic thought tickled Matt's conscience. Why, if Tyler and Chrissi were already lovers with a baby on the way, why would his father want Matt to know that she'd been tucked away in guest room with him as a chaperone? Something was off – it didn't make sense.

Matt had already begun to admit that he hadn't been fair to Chrissi last night and now he was starting to question his reactions to Tyler. But he was unable to imagine himself forgiving his friend for leading his little sister down this path – at least not yet.

"I love you, Matt," Ashley was saying. "But I'm afraid your actions have been way out of line in this case. You've let your sister down, you've turned against your friend and you abandoned me."

He'd begun to feel the sting of shame for his behavior, even before this encounter with Ashley. That's the reason he'd gone to her office, to seek her out and apologize. "I know," he said roughly. "I'm sorry I stayed away last night."

Ashley growled in frustration and disbelief as she spun and began striding toward her own vehicle, a tired Trailblazer that had come with the purchase of the town's newspaper. Just as she reached for the door handle, Matt's arm shot past her. His hand pressed against the door frame assuring that she wouldn't be able to wrench the door open.

"I said I was sorry," he began in a quiet tone that he battled to keep from escalating. "Why are you still upset?"

He was rewarded with an icy glare. "You have three big issues to resolve here," she said. "And you start making amends on the one of lowest priority."

Ashley closed her eyes and counted to ten, and then back to one, before she opened them again. Looking up into her husband's crystal blue eyes, she saw that he really didn't get it. They hadn't been married all that long, and Ashley figured they both had some learning to do.

"You're missing my point," she began and Matt's scowl deepened. "But I have a feeling that I'm missing yours, too."

"There's a chance," he agreed. "You are not my lowest priority. You are my first priority. No matter what else is going on, I shouldn't have left you alone last night. It was immature and irrational." He tried to kiss her again, but she dodged the advance. "It was selfish. It was wrong. And I am sorry."

"I appreciate that, and I won't stay upset about that. This time. But what about the others? You hurt them more deeply than you hurt me," she argued.

"I will talk to them, but they aren't here right now," he explained slowly. She let herself be pulled back into his embrace as he continued speaking. "I will make things right with them. But the most important thing is to work this out with you." She did let him kiss her then.

"I'm your first priority?" she asked in a quiet plea for affirmation.

"Absolutely," he asserted solemnly. The truce with his wife would buy him some time to figure out how to approach his sister. And his friend.

But the comfort was cut short, when Ashley spoke again. "When are you going to talk to Chrissi?"

"Later," he growled as he tried to curb his frustration. Softening, he added, "Right now I'm busy trying to console my wife. Win back her affections."

She tipped her face upward and accepted a tender kiss from the man she loved. "What about Tyler?" she persisted.

"Can we go home and discuss this? Maybe we'll even feel like making up later." He waggled his eyebrows suggestively, causing Ashley to burst into laughter. Matt grew serious again. "I'll meet you at home?" he asked as he opened the door of the Trailblazer.

She agreed, but added that she would need to swing past the office and lock up before she met him back at the house.

Matt had learned early in their married life that Ashley was a sucker for a grilled or broiled steak, herbed potatoes and cheesecake. Armed with that knowledge, he'd made a quick supply run at the family-run grocery store and taken the first

119

steps that he hoped would lead to earning her forgiveness. By the time Ashley arrived home, Matt had the supper preparations well underway.

"Good news!" she crowed as she entered the kitchen. "Oh, that smells delicious," she said, changing tacks. She piled her bag on a chair in the living room and dropped her jacket over it. "I'm famished!"

"What's the news?"

She explained that upon returning to the office, Ashley had discovered that the sheriff had left a message that he had obtained a warrant for the arrest of Adam Brewer. The man would be charged with illegal entry and burglary based on the evidence at the Chronicle, his finger prints on a railing outside the building and the statement of a witness. "I'll bet that's the reason Bobbie didn't come to work today," she theorized.

"She could be sick," Matt interjected.

"She would have called," Ashley asserted as she lifted the lid from the cheesecake to steal a taste.

"How do you know she would have?"

"How do you know she wouldn't have?"

"You shouldn't assume things," Matt said sternly.

"You assume things," she countered smartly.

"Like what?" he demanded. "I'm very open-minded."

Ashley bit her lip rather than blurt out a reference to the events of the preceding evening. She looked up into his face, batted her eyes and demurely delivered her reply, "Whatever you say, dear."

"So you really think Bobbie would quit just because her son may have broken into the Chronicle," he asked in an open attempt to change the subject. "Seems crazy."

"I don't know," Ashley replied as she began to set the table. "Guess what?"

"I've no idea. Maybe your ADHD is acting up?" Matt ventured.

"We might be sued!" she said cheerily.

"We? Who?"

"We ... the newspaper," she supplied. "Isn't it grand?"

Matt pulled Ashley close, delivered a quick kiss and informed her that he had married the oddest publisher in the state. And, while he held her still, in all seriousness he asked who would want to sue her and for what reason.

"Oh, there were complaints from both sides after we published the story about the cheese factory's upcoming expansion," she explained. "But the actual threat came from Evan Davis – one of the lower management guys at the plant. He seems to feel he's been violated somehow."

Matt's concern deepened at the words. "Didn't Charlie and Catherine have trouble with him a while back?" He seemed to recall that the Davis character had filed suit over another story that had been published several months earlier. "Maybe you should just keep a lawyer on retainer?"

Matt delivered the food to the table and held out a chair for Ashley to be seated.

"That's the reason Mason was in my office today – he was reviewing Shelby's notes and the tape of her interviews for the story," Ashley explained.

"And holding my wife," Matt added coldly.

They seemed to be circling back to the serious topics, so she decided to just say what was on her mind. "He told me you were upset and I started to cry a little," she explained. "I'm sorry that it happened, but it was nothing - just brotherly support. He said I reminded him of his sister, Katie."

Matt flushed and his expression darkened in response to her easy words. "That's a load," he attested.

"I beg your pardon?"

"Have you ever been a man?" He glared accusingly at his wife.

"You're crazed."

"A man cannot hold a woman and think about his sister at the same time," Matt explained. He spoke each word separately as if to help clarify his meaning. "It does not work that way."

"But -"

"Not ever," he barked.

She ate quietly for a few minutes - a fact that struck Matt as odd. Maybe he'd missed something. Was he supposed to say something? Was he in trouble again? Still?

"Ashley?"

Nothing.

"Honey?"

They both finished the meal and Ashley began clearing the table. Matt joined her and they worked quietly. When they finished, Matt ventured into conversation. "I thought we were okay, but now you're mad again."

"You don't believe me," she countered sadly. "About Mason."

"I believe *you* believe Mason," he explained. "But *I* don't believe Mason."

Confusion pulled at her brows, "What?"

A deep sigh escaped from Matt's lips. How to explain? "When I hold you, and you hold me, what do you think about?"

Thankfully, Ashley's skin flushed pink. She stammered but didn't really reveal the answer.

"Do you think of Tom or Scott?" he asked quietly, referring to her brothers. "Do you think 'Oh, hey. Matt's a lot like Tom? Or Scott and Matt are the same height – I sure miss Scott right now?'"

"Don't be crazy!"

"Alright then," Matt declared. "Trust me on this. Mason was *not* thinking of his sister."

CHAPTER TWELVE

Sandy grit irritated the tender tissue at the corner of his eye as Tyler scratched a hand over his face. The alarm clock had pulled him none too gently from his afternoon sleep. Rubbing his eyes again, he focused on the readout of the clock and learned he had plenty of time before he needed to get ready for the Wednesday evening activities at church.

He'd been on the ambulance crew from midnight Tuesday, after leaving Chrissi in his father's care, until noon Wednesday. The shift had been an easy one. He and his partner had responded to a car accident on the interstate, transporting a single individual to the local hospital; assisted an elderly person who had fallen in his home, and made a transfer from the care center for the elderly to a larger hospital in Sioux Falls.

Mrs. Holmes had been delighted that Tyler had stopped in to visit her before he had headed home at the end of his shift. Her health was improving and, she'd informed him optimistically, she planned to be able to return to her own home the following week. She'd asked if he had read the book yet, and he'd replied that he hadn't picked it up yet.

"Why not?" she demanded shrewdly. Pinning him with a hard glare, she asked, "What changed? I thought you were all worked up over the past ..."

He shrugged in response, but when she continued to wait for an answer, he added, "I will read it. I promise." Tyler had risen and kissed her cheek, before he added mildly, "Somehow the future now seems more important than the past."

Bony, cold fingers caught his face and she inspected him closely, and very seriously. "That's good to hear," she finally said. "I'm happy for you."

The house was empty when Tyler returned to his father's home a short time later. Chrissi was at school, and presumably would be spending this night either in her own apartment or would be a guest in her mother's home. And Jeff was nowhere to be found, but Tyler was certain that his father had begun slipping into the office for a few hours each day. Rehabilitation time wasn't sitting well with the senior Schuster, and from his comments, Tyler surmised the retirement plan had been rescheduled by a few years.

Tyler stretched as he rose from the bed, once again brushing a hand across his face. Yawning, he rubbed at his eyes again. It was then that Tyler recalled that when he was a little boy, his dad had referred to the overnight buildup as eye boogies. A sleepy smile crept onto his face as Tyler thought about teaching his own child silly terms a few years down the road. Regardless of the baby's gender, he would also teach the child life skills like hunting and fishing, how to get along with people, the importance of hard work and Christian faith. Shaking his head, Tyler laughed to himself as he headed toward the kitchen – those were mighty big goals considering the child in question was currently smaller than his own fist.

The radio played softly in the room he'd just left, but he wasn't hearing it over the sudden pounding of the pulse in his ears. A baby! Chrissi's baby! His focus locked on his clenched fist, as his mind tried to make the abstract thought of a baby into a firm reality. He had confidently told Chrissi that he loved her and that he would love the baby as his own, but what if he couldn't? What if it didn't happen that way? What if he held the baby looked into the tiny being's face and felt nothing – or worse yet – revulsion?

Panic seared a swath through Tyler's mind; they could be making a monumental mistake. Marrying because of pregnancy was probably a mistake. But then a consoling peacefulness spread through Tyler's mind and he asked himself if the reason he'd proposed really was the pregnancy. And his heart answered the question with a resounding "no". The reason he'd proposed was because he had wanted to; the pregnancy had only been a catalyst. It had changed Chrissi's life and opened up the option of her staying in Miller's Bend, because going on to college would be very difficult for her as a single mother.

What Tyler felt for Chrissi was love. His feelings were deep and true and pure. And he understood with renewed confidence that her child would be his – in his heart and in reality. His attention riveted again on his clenched fist, Tyler wondered if the child was indeed that size. Chrissi was through one trimester. Could the babe's presence be felt by placing a hand over the womb that cradled him or her at this point in development? Would Chrissi allow him to touch her abdomen – to feel the child within? A fresh excitement washed over Tyler as he began to wonder whether the baby's movements could be felt at this early stage of development. Could Tyler begin to bond with him or her by spending time with Chrissi?

Tyler's thoughts were interrupted as the back door opened slowly. Chrissi called cautiously, "Anybody here?"

"Yeah," he answered with a sleep-roughened voice. "I'm here."

She peeked around the edge of the door, her cheeks flushed slightly, her eyes shy. "I didn't know if I should knock …"

He stepped to the entrance and opened the door wide, cupped her elbow and encouraged her to come inside. "No need. You're family now," he said with reverence reverberating deep within. "My family."

Stark longing shown in her expressive cocoa colored eyes, but to Tyler's frustration it wasn't the kind of longing one might expected from a fiancée. Even though she cast her glance away, Tyler read her need for reassurance.

Dread clutched at Tyler and he reached for her. "What's wrong?" he demanded a little too harshly.

"I was wondering …" she began, but her words faltered. He waited while she paced around the kitchen. She faced him squarely, lifted her chin and braced her hands on her hips. "Are you sure?" she finally voiced the question she'd been battling. And then the image of the warrior woman faded and in a pleading whisper she repeated, "Are you sure you want me?"

The stark vulnerability written in Chrissi's eyes nearly broke Tyler's heart. How could he offer her the reassurance she needed? Precious moments earlier he'd been the one who was questioning their decision and now he needed to defend their plan to her.

"Yes, Chris." Even though he spoke quietly, they both heard the tremor in his voice. "I am sure." He moved close and clasped her hands in his own, and noted distractedly that her fingers were bare. Why wasn't she wearing the ring he'd slipped onto her finger the previous evening? His spirit ached to hold her close, but his mind cautioned not to demand that of her. Releasing her hands, he opened his arms in invitation, and she hesitated. "The feelings I have for you have been with me for a long time," he confessed. "It's not like I found out you were pregnant and then thought 'Oh hey, Chris is in a bind and I can help her out'."

Hope flickered in her eyes as she listened. "I've denied my love for you because you were young, and you would be going off to college," he continued. "But this pregnancy has upset your plans. I didn't want to be the influence that derailed your dreams. But now -"

At hearing his words, Chrissi's demeanor changed, but not in a good way. "Derailed?" she demanded with an accusation gleaming in her eye. "You want to marry me because my plans were derailed?"

Heat rose in his cheeks as the realization of how badly his explanation had gone. "No. I want to marry you because I love you," he asserted. More gently he added, "And you love me."

Unease tripped along his spine when she didn't immediately respond. He waited, hoping for the best.

Chrissi's nostrils flared as she inhaled before challenging him, "What if I told you that I still plan to go to college?"

His response was out before Tyler had time to mentally run through the options. "Then I would go with you." The answer had surprised him, and clearly Chrissi had noticed.

"Would you?" She narrowed her gaze on him as if expecting he would grow a second head or burst into flames as retribution for lying.

"Yes. Absolutely."

"How?"

"What?"

"How would you go with me? You own a business here … Your friends are here … Your family is here …" The challenge was back in her voice now, but Tyler detected another quality – an uncertainty – as if she was asking for a promise of some sort.

He regarded her a moment longer before understanding that she was seeking confirmation that he would back her through life, even if it pushed him out of his comfort zone. He sighed, but answered earnestly. "I would need more than a few seconds to work out the details. But yes, I would go with you. I can sell the business or hire a manager. I can get a job in Sioux Falls or a nearby community. I can stay in touch with my friends, or, believe it or not, I am able to make new friends," he said with a smile.

"But most importantly," he continued, as his fingers lovingly skimmed her cheek and his gaze locked on Chrissi's. "You are my family. You and our baby."

The rich brown eyes, amber eyes when the light hit them right, or when they were filling up with tears, scrutinized him. Chrissi's expression softened after a moment longer. "That was beautiful. And I believe you mean it," she responded. Chrissi's smile spread slowly, and as it did, a warmth spread through Tyler's heart as well.

The relief at hearing Tyler's reassurance calmed the questions that had been pinging around in Chrissi's mind. She'd been questioning herself and him, and their mutual decision to wed. She couldn't focus on her schoolwork and had rushed to Jeff's house as soon as she'd been able. She'd hoped she would find Tyler; and she'd hoped she wouldn't.

But when he'd responded to her call before she had stepped inside, the familiarity of his voice had pushed her roiling emotions away from fear and toward excitement. He'd met her at the door – no, he'd greeted her – welcoming her home. And that act, in and of itself, had begun to allay her fears. He was genuinely happy to see her.

She'd needed to know, though, so she'd asked whether he was sure. And once again he had assured her that the reason he'd proposed was his feelings – their feelings – not the baby. Several times now he had referred to her pregnancy as "our baby", and it bolstered her confidence each time she heard the words.

Chrissi thought of girls she knew who would play games with guys, teasing them, taunting them, tricking them into saying things. There were girls who tried through various deceptions and schemes to get the boys to pledge their love. "I'm not messing with you, Ty," she said quietly. "I'm not just trying to get you to tell me you love me. I'm scared that we might be making a mistake."

"I know." His voice was ragged when he continued, "I know you, Chris. You're not a person who plays games with people. You have legitimate concerns. I have concerns of my own." She let herself be pulled into his embrace and waited. "We will have to work our way through them, but when love is the foundation, we will build a strong and secure marriage. An enduring marriage."

"I want that," she responded quietly.

Tyler pulled back so he could see her expression, and once again clasped her hands in his. "What is it you want?"

She seemed shy again, as if answering honestly was revealing too much of her own heart. "I only plan to marry once, Ty. I want it to be forever. I want a love – a relationship – that endures and prospers and flourishes. I want a marriage that lasts and is rewarding to both parties."

Strange sensations fluttered in Chrissi's stomach in response to the soul-searching gaze from Tyler. It was embarrassing, having him look at her as though he could see inside her heart, her mind, her very being. Chrissi wasn't sure how it happened, but seconds later his hands had glided up her arms, tickled across the ridge of her shoulders and along her neck. Strong and rough, but gentle, they cupped her face as he moved nearer, and nearer still.

His searing gaze never wavered from her own eyes; never let her glance away, as their hearts seemed to meld. Her heart raced, her skin burned at his touch, and without realizing what she was about to do, Chrissi shifted closer. Her senses were taking it all in and when she felt the caress of his breath on her lips, she was drawn to touch him.

Although she willed her own hands to stay obediently at her sides, she now noticed in a detached sort of way, that one rested on his ribcage and the other was at his throat registering the pulse pounding beneath the skin. The rebellious limb found the scratchy jawline, memorizing the form of her beloved's face, feeling the muscle beneath bunch and relax. And at long last – but much too soon – her delicate fingers found the soft skin of Tyler's lips.

His breath stopped, as if he feared that moving or even breathing would frighten her away. But fear was the farthest thing from Chrissi's mind. Emboldened, she moved her fingers away from the tender skin and hesitantly touched the spot they'd abandoned with her own lips.

For a second they both stayed stock still, frozen by emotions. And then Ty pulled back just a fraction and drew a long breath. Their lips met again, but at Tyler's initiation. Chrissi felt caution in his touch. She felt her own response becoming bolder, and a moment later, it was Tyler who backed away. "Have mercy," he whispered.

After an awkward moment, she asked with more confidence, "You don't think there's something wrong with me for questioning what we are doing?"

"Not at all," Tyler replied. He shifted Chrissi away from his body and cupped her face. Earnest gray eyes locked on hers before he spoke. "Even in the Bible it says something about men preparing to build up towers; it asks who wouldn't first sit down and count the cost, whether he has enough to complete it." When she would have spoken, he silenced her with the light touch of a fingertip to her lips. The seriousness in his expression was replaced with playfulness. "And no, I don't mean I see a cost in our relationship. I mean that the Bible encourages us to be thoughtful and deliberate about our actions and our decisions."

She stepped closer to him, intertwined her fingers between his, but then, she didn't seem to know what to do next. Chrissi released the hold on him and turned, thinking she might grab a quick snack before heading to the church. A strange noise originated deep in Tyler's throat, halting Chrissi's retreat; she paused and turned to face him, silently questioning what he was up to.

"I … um." His voice cracked as the words wouldn't come.

She waited, wondering why the man who was normally so calm and comfortable seemed to be nervous and uncertain.

He tried again. "Can I … I mean would it be alright …"

Tyler's awkwardness lightened the mood – at least from Chrissi's point of view, and a slight giggle escaped her lips. His expression seemed strained in response. And she apologized for laughing. "I'm just not used to seeing you tongue-tied when you have something to say," she explained.

"It's not funny," he refuted. His skin had reddened from his obvious nervous embarrassment. "This is serious."

Chrissi couldn't stop her smile from expanding until she heard the rest of his words.

"Can you feel the baby yet?" he finally blurted. "Could I feel, if I …" The words had died away again and his face flamed a brilliant red. His focus dropped to Chrissi's mid-section. She could only guess what he had in mind from that.

"What?" she faltered. "If you what?" Her eyes were as big as silver dollars as she looked at him incredulously.

His hands were up as if to fend off an anticipated attack. "Hold on, now … I only wondered if I could touch your stomach," he offered in a placating tone. A look of wonder crept into his expression as his focus locked again on Chrissi's face. "Can you feel her move yet?"

As if mesmerized, she returned to his side and reached for his hand. His skin felt warm and rough against her tender abdomen as she guided him to the small firm knot that until that moment, only she had felt. The tension in his body relaxed a bit as he inhaled. Tyler's acceptance and open caring for the baby bought tears to Chrissi's eyes. She remembered that he'd asked whether the baby's movements could be felt. Belatedly she responded, "I haven't felt him moving yet. They say first time mothers don't usually feel movement until around 18 weeks."

A profound sense of wonder wound through Tyler's mind and wrapped snugly around his heart. He yearned to stay just like this until the life beneath his hand could make its presence known by tickling his hand. Reality of course would prevent such behavior. Reluctantly, he pulled his hand away from the silken softness of the skin he touched. "Thank you," he breathed.

CHAPTER THIRTEEN

Tyler sat in his pickup, staring at the lighted windows of Melanie Gibson's apartment, steadying his thoughts for the next family discussion. It had only been one day since Chrissi had revealed her pregnancy to her family. Only one day since Tyler had intervened to redirect her brother's surprised anger away from her. It was a tactic which had worked amazingly well.

They were meeting again tonight at her mother's apartment, where Chrissi planned to live until Mrs. Holmes' release from the hospital. Tyler's father had been invited by Chrissi, but he'd declined. "You kids will be fine," he'd said to the two of them. "I'm proud of the way you both are handling this. It's my understanding that you plan to tell them the whole story, and I'm willing to respect that." He'd paused so long that Tyler thought he was through speaking, but then he added, "It's a huge undertaking – trying to decide what's best for a soul entrusted to you – be sure to consider what would be best for the child, not simply what is easiest on your own consciences." Jeff's brow furrowed as he considered whether to say more, but in the end he simply added, "If you change your mind, and decide to keep it among the three of us, I can abide by that as well. Just let me know how it goes tonight."

The shadow of a man crossed behind the closed curtains, and then a woman's shape joined the other shadow. Chrissi's parents, Byron and Melanie, had been estranged for 16 years. It was Chrissi's disappearance after Christmas that had brought Byron to Miller's Bend, and he had stayed in town after her return. And now her parents were working to restore a relationship. Byron had been adamant about staying near enough to assist Melanie as she continued taking treatments for cancer.

Tyler's mind wandered to the conversation between Chrissi and himself in his father's house a few short hours earlier. The idea of the two of them as a couple was so fresh that it hadn't really solidified in Chrissi's mind. It probably hadn't solidified in her heart either. It was his fear that she'd be swayed to take a different course than the one they'd chosen together. *Lord, I hope she's ready for this conversation with her family*, he prayed silently.

Suddenly the truck rocked to the left a milli-second before a deafening drumbeat rang from the roof above. Tyler jumped in his seat, twisting to glare out the driver's side window at the assaulting offender. The door was jerked open and there stood Matt.

"Cripes, man!" Tyler wheezed. "You trying to give me a heart attack?"

A wicked smile spread across his friend's face and he shrugged as if it was nothing. "I really wanted to get back at you for the years you took off my life last night," he explained lamely. "And since you don't have a sister ..."

Ashley appeared out of nowhere, delivering a sound slap to Matt's chest. His grin turned sheepish as he wrapped an arm around her shoulder.

Cautiously Tyler asked, "So you're over the urge to kill me?"

"For now," the taller man replied. His blue eyes held some humor now, but there was still a hint of sadness lingering. He scraped a hand across his face before he added, "I still can't believe this is happening. But, I guess it could be worse."

Tyler bit back the words that played in his mind: *It IS worse.* Instead he thought of the fledgling love he and Chrissi felt for each other and smiled. He thought of the feelings that had swelled within him as he'd touched the spot where the child rested, nestled safely inside a woman filled with God's love. "Yeah, it's alright, and it's getting better every day," he admitted.

Tyler had stepped down from the truck and before he closed the door, Ashley handed him a bundle of papers. It was Mrs. Holmes' book, he presumed. He placed it on the bench seat behind the driver's seat. The three walked into the apartment, up the steps to the second floor, and down the long corridor in silence. Tyler remembered the loss he'd felt when he noticed Chrissi hadn't been wearing the ring he'd given her. It was his mother's ring and he wondered if Chrissi knew the significance of his gift.

He'd asked her about it while at church that evening, and she'd replied that she was keeping it close to her heart. Her delicate hand had patted her chest, below her neckline, to emphasize the point. He hadn't noticed the fine gold chain she wore before that, and figured she'd placed the ring on the necklace. "I don't want to wear it publicly until we talk with my family again," she'd whispered.

Now, as the trio approached the apartment door, his father's words had been niggling at Tyler. Chrissi had seemed adamant about telling her family members what had happened. But they were still reeling from the surprise of Chrissi's pregnancy and the shock of Tyler's implied role. How would they react to hearing that Chrissi and Tyler had deceived them by letting them – no leading them – to believe Tyler had fathered the child. And how would they accept the baby when he or she arrived?

Perhaps, he thought, there was good reason to be less than forthright about the events leading to the current situation. And then something clicked in his mind. Maybe Tyler's own father and Mrs. Holmes had good reason for hiding his own heritage from him – and from the townspeople. If they were to reveal the whole truth to Chrissi's family, then what? If each person confided to one friend, how fast would the story spread? Tyler would probably tell Riley as well, Riley would share the news with Shelby, and maybe Andrew. If they each told one person, and so on, the whole town would know in a matter of days. How would her friends, her teachers, or even strangers regard Chrissi once word got around?

Matt knocked on his mother's apartment door, and it was opened quickly. Melanie's expression lit with happiness as she let her gaze encompass the trio in the hallway. "Well, isn't this a nice surprise," she said warmly. "Come on in."

Matt rolled his eyes in response, and asked, "What surprise, Mom? You knew Chrissi invited us over." He bent and kissed the cheek of the woman he had always adored.

"The surprise is that you and Tyler arrived together," she said pointedly. "The last time you were together, I was afraid I'd need to call Jeff to come over and break it up."

Matt's skin colored as he remembered the scene. "I'm sorry about that, Mom," he said quietly.

"Don't tell me, son. It's your sister you owe the apology to," she reprimanded. Her gaze shifted from Matt to Tyler when she added, "And your best friend." With that, she clasped Ashley's hand and pulled her toward the kitchen, "Can you give me your advice on something?" she asked as they walked away.

"I'm 28 years old; I'm an aspiring artist; I'm a married man, and she still thinks she can tell me what to do," Matt muttered good-naturedly as he slid his jacket off his shoulders and hung it on a peg. Tyler did the same.

"She doesn't do it as often as she used to," Tyler answered with a sad smile. "I'm sorry about the way it went last night, buddy."

"I am, too," Matt admitted. "I was way out of line." They regarded each other silently a moment, before Matt added, "But I'm still upset."

"No doubt," Tyler answered. "And I still love your sister."

Byron, Chrissi's father, had been talking with her about Maddy, the cousin she had gone to Chicago to try to save. Something about Maddy wanting to move to Miller's Bend, but Chrissi was listening with only half her mind. Instead she had been seated on the couch in the living room of the small apartment dreading the moment when Ty and Matt would meet again. She'd envisioned the two men she loved duking it out, or at the very least, having another heated argument. So to say she was shocked when they entered the room side by side, joking about something mundane, was a serious understatement.

She rose from the cushion as her instinct urged her to go to Tyler, but her mind directed her to her brother. Confused, she looked from one to the other. "It's okay, Chrissi," Matt's voice rumbled reassuringly. He extended an arm, welcoming her into his embrace, but she hesitated, looking to Ty for a clue. He smiled and nodded slightly, so she went to Matt.

Matt held her in the loose circle of his arms. It was an act he'd done so many times throughout her life, and the tenderness of his embrace and the bittersweet quality of the memories had her crying in no time. Matt's father had died when he was only eight years old, their mother had subsequently married Byron, and soon after they'd had Chrissi. But Byron had left them when she was only two. Even though the siblings were ten years apart in age, they'd been remarkably close, and the effect of Matt's reaction yesterday had wounded her deeply.

Matt noticed the unspoken exchange between his sister and his friend, and snorted. "She's already looking to you instead of me," he mumbled in Tyler's direction.

Shaking his head and smiling, Tyler gestured toward Chrissi and refuted the statement, "Right. Look who she's clinging to."

"You can take her," Matt countered. "She's getting my shirt all wet." His actions belied his words though, as he held Chrissi lovingly in his arms, reluctant to release her to anyone else. Then very quietly, he spoke the words to Chrissi that would help begin to heal the wounds he'd inflicted the night before. "I'm sorry, Chrissi. I let you down yesterday; I promise I won't do it again. I'm here for you and I always will be."

Ashley nudged Chrissi. "Hey, why don't you hang on to your own man," she ribbed, "and let me have mine back." Chrissi sniffled and met her sister-in-law's teasing expression, replying without words, she smiled, and felt the bond with the other woman deepening. "We're all here for you," Ashley added as she squeezed Chrissi's hand.

And then Chrissi found herself pulled tightly into Tyler's arms – too tightly. She panicked and stiffened as an instinctive reaction swirled in her gut. Almost simultaneously, he relaxed his hold and whispered, "Sorry. You okay?" She inhaled deeply and exhaled slowly as her gaze met his. She nodded nearly imperceptibly and forced her muscles to soften and her mind to calm. She didn't dare look to her family members to gauge their responses to her actions.

"Tyler. Chrissi," Matt began to speak, drawing everyone's attention. "I have been informed by my wife," he paused to kiss Ashley's forehead. "My mother," he continued, raising a hand to gesture in Melanie's direction, "And my step-father," he said with a nod toward Byron, "that I was a complete idiot last night."

No one refuted the statement. "It wasn't really a revelation, but you don't all have to be in unanimous agreement," Matt joked. The seriousness was back in his voice when he spoke again, directing his comments to Chrissi and Tyler. "I was so surprised and angry ... I ... I just ... I guess I wasn't thinking straight. After you left, Ashley read me the riot act."

Byron had moved to Melanie's side and guided her to the couch where he joined her. The two young couples remained standing as if there might be a need for action. Ashley was tucked under Matt's arm; Chrissi was close beside Tyler, his arm draped casually behind her back, hand resting at her waist. Ashley reached for Chrissi's hand again and squeezed it in an unspoken gesture of solidarity.

Matt's voice faltered as he continued, "I'm sorry that I reacted like a ... a -"

"Neanderthal?" a feminine voice filled in for him when he stalled.

Matt smiled. "Thank you," he said without looking at the speaker. "I behaved in a way that was -"

"Primitive?"

"Reactionary?"

"Unreasonable?"

It seemed that all the women had ideas about his behavior. Matt was thankful when Tyler came to his assistance, raising his hands to stop the increasing onslaught of helpful terminology. "Alright, ladies," Tyler said. "I think he understands." Then looking to his friend's face, Tyler offered, "I really can't say I wouldn't have reacted the same way – or worse if the situation was reversed."

"Thanks." Matt paced away from Ashley before turning to look again at his sister and his friend. They looked good together; as if being together made each of them a stronger, better version of themselves. Maybe they should be together – as if he had any say in that! Matt did have more to say though.

"I spent the night alone at my studio because I was stubborn and felt insulted that Ashley had sided with you," he said to the couple. "Sometime in the night while I was paging through the Bible, I came across a verse that resonated with me. It advised, 'Know this, my beloved brothers: let every person be quick to hear, slow to speak, slow to anger; for the anger of man does not produce the righteousness of God,'" Matt cited a verse from the book of James. "I guess I became self-righteous last night, rather than reflecting the love of God. And for that I apologize. Again."

"Your news was a big shock to us all," Melanie directed her comment to her daughter.

Chrissi's dark eyes were pulled to Tyler as she responded, "Oh, I think we all had some surprises last night."

"I'm … I'm happy for you, honey. You're going to be a wonderful mother." Melanie's eyes grew misty, as she added, "And I get to have a grandbaby to spoil."

"I'm sure you'll have lots of grandbabies to spoil," Matt interjected with a sly grin.

His reward was the stinging of a pinch from Ashley, who smiled sweetly and added, "But not for a long time."

Chrissi fidgeted in Tyler's embrace and he figured she was working up to dropping the real bombshell. When her gaze flickered to his and then darted away, he saw the fear and resignation in her expression. She was going to tell the whole unsavory truth because that's what they had agreed to before they'd thought through all the potentially devastating impacts. Before his father's warning words to do what is best for the child, not to do what's easiest on your own conscience. "There's more you need to know," she said with ominous foreshadowing. "More …"

The look of misery and dread in Chrissi's bearing pushed Tyler to intercede without conscious thought. His hand captured her hand and rubbed the spot where his ring should be resting. Touching her cheek gently with his other hand and attempting to get her to shift gears, his gaze caught on hers. He wanted to scream "Don't do it! Don't say it out loud!" but he couldn't.

Chrissi's words caught in her throat, lodged there for some reason, refusing to flow forth. Tyler's hand on hers was a gentle reminder that she'd hidden his ring away from the world and now he had stopped her from beginning the horrible tale of how she really came to be pregnant. Confused, she searched his eyes, hoping to understand what he was doing. She needed to get this over with so she could curl up and start healing all over again. But she dreaded it. Dreaded guessing how her family would react; or, for that matter, how strangers would react. How would people treat the baby after they knew he or she was the product of a violent act? How does a child deal with the knowledge that he wasn't created out of an act of love?

Tyler's cheek brushed against Chrissi's as he leaned close and whispered for her hearing only, "Trust me." She felt his fingers at the clasp of the necklace as he worked to free the ring that dangled near her heart. When he had liberated the ring, he stepped back from Chrissi, and suddenly she could breathe again.

The buzzing in her ears almost drowned out his words as he addressed her family members. "Chrissi and I have already done this, but I thought you'd like to be witnesses to our commitment to each other," he explained. And then he turned toward her and those beautiful gray eyes locked on hers. His expression was soft and warm with emotion, but she also detected a hint of warning – he wanted her to follow his lead.

He dropped his focus for a moment as if seeking guidance, and then lowered himself to one knee. When Tyler raised his face to look up at Chrissi, the emotions there stole her breath. "I love you Chris," he said with reverberating reverence. "I have admired you, appreciated your drive and your intelligence. I've been awestruck by your loving, giving nature. I've envied your faith and your family. I've been captivated by your sense of humor; confused by your commitment that everyone should be treated openly and fairly regardless of who they are, where they come from and what they've done. You are truly a magnificent person and I'd be honored to build a life together with you." He paused and Chrissi saw the truth in his eyes – he was pledging himself to her and asking that she do the same for him.

Tears streaked her cheeks as she realized that she could let herself trust in Tyler and believe he would be there for her, loving her, taking care of her, partnering with her for all of their Earthly days. She truly could rely on him. She already did, but simply hadn't acknowledged the fact until now. "Oh, Ty," she sighed.

"Chris," he said, "Will you honor me by allowing me to be your husband? Trust me to love you and take care of you? And promise to love me and take care of me in return? Let us live, laugh and love as a complete and happy family in the eyes of the world and in the eyes of God. Will you marry me?"

The vision of Tyler, kneeling there before her, was all wavy as the tears in Chrissi's eyes distorted the picture. She nodded, while trying to dash away the wetness from her cheeks. Suddenly, he was standing, holding her gently, and enfolding her in his love. "These are happy tears?" he asked.

She nodded again as a wad of tissues appeared in her hand. When Chrissi had recovered, Tyler took her hand in his, and held the ring that she'd worn on the necklace. "This ring was my mother's," he began to speak, but stopped when his voice cracked. He cleared his throat. And cleared it again. "This ring was my mother's. And as you know, she died when I was little. I don't remember everything about her, but I know that she and Dad loved each other far more deeply than I could understand at the time. Looking back, I know they had the commitment to each other, coupled with their faith that allowed them to open their hearts to everything that came to them. I hope that we can follow their example and form a household where there is abundant, welcoming, enriching love for all."

The words probably sounded sweet and flowery to those gathered around, but to Chrissi, they were much more. Tyler's words were a pledge of love and commitment. He'd said the words straight out the previous evening – that he would love the baby as if it were his own. But tonight, although her family didn't understand the real message, he'd solemnly promised to follow his father's example of love. How could Chrissi reply?

"I …" she began. "I feel so overwhelmed," she said with a wavering smile. "You've been in my heart for a long time, too." Chrissi drew a shaky breath before she continued. "I thought it was just a crush; I thought I was too young to experience real love." She didn't look away from Tyler's face when she added, "There are others who might think that too. But I'm glad you took the chance to show me now how you feel. That selfless move let me acknowledge my feelings for you. I will try to be worthy of your love, and I will endeavor to match your commitment to our family."

She realized that the words they'd spoken to each other had deepened the pretense that Ty was indeed the father of her child. They'd given roots to the lie; they'd committed to nurturing the image they'd created. And oddly, Chrissi was filled with relief as she pulled herself more tightly against Tyler's chest. They stood together like that for only seconds before they were engulfed in hugs from the family. They had more talking to do, but they'd committed to a course now and although they hadn't planned on the evening working out this way, each of them felt at peace with the end result.

CHAPTER FOURTEEN

"You know," Mason informed his friends who had gathered for lunch at the family-style restaurant a couple weeks later. "Katie will graduate in May with a degree in business. Maybe she's the answer to your problem."

"What problem?" Erik asked as stepped next to Mason's left side. The sheriff had been dining with a deputy when he'd seen Mason, Tyler, Riley and Matt at a table in the middle of the dining area. He approached while they waited for their orders to arrive.

"Join us?" Mason invited, with a nod toward an empty chair.

"I already ate," he replied, gesturing toward the deputy who stood near the till. "Just wanted to see how things are going. I hear your dad's back at work full-time?" he directed toward Tyler.

"Yep. He was going crazy at home. Like a caged animal," Tyler confirmed. "He's glad to be back at the station."

"It's a relief to have him at the helm again," the other man asserted. Tyler simply nodded. Turning his attention to Mason, Erik repeated his question, "So who's got a problem? And how can your sister help?"

Erik's assessing gaze followed the three men as they glanced at Tyler who squirmed slightly. "I need to hire a

149

manager for the nursery," he replied. Then looking to Mason, he added, "It's not a big deal."

Despite having declined the offer to join them, Erik claimed the empty chair. "It's not going to work," Riley contributed. "You can't operate business from a distance. If I tried that, productivity would drop drastically." Riley had purchased a floundering metal fabrication company years earlier and turned it around with intense management and innovative ideas.

"It's not like I'll be in Timbuktu," Tyler's exasperation was rising. "We'll be in Sioux Falls. It's only a couple hours away."

Matt was shaking his head at the idea, but it was Riley who voiced the next concern. "It won't matter. You'll be busy with a new job, new wife and new baby. You're not going to be running up here to check on your business. I hate to say it, but you'd be better off to sell."

"Baby?" Erik asked with mild disbelief. Then looking to Riley, he added, "It's a good thing I didn't fall for your wife's matchmaking attempt." He slapped a hand to Tyler's shoulder before adding, "Congratulations."

"Thanks." Pride colored Tyler's voice as he responded.

"You could make Chrissi change her plans," Mason suggested. "Stay here in Miller's Bend and make a life."

Both married men laughed aloud in response.

"You can't do that to Chrissi," Matt finally contributed from beside Mason. "She's dreamed of being a nurse since she could walk." His expression grew serious as he speared Tyler with his gaze and an undercurrent of warning zinged between the two friends. "You can't take that away from her."

Tyler's expression hardened at hearing Matt's message. They'd been through this before. "I've told you that's not my intention."

"Sometimes intentions get screwed up by reality," Matt countered. "She needs to get her education. She deserves to follow her dreams."

They were silent as the waitress delivered their orders. She looked questioningly to the sheriff, but he shook his head. The soles of her shoes squeaked as she hurried back to the kitchen to retrieve another order for a nearby table.

Erik cleared his throat before asking, "So how can your sister help?"

"Like I said, she'll have a business degree in a few more weeks," he replied to Erik's question, but Mason's focus was on Tyler. "She's got experience in a greenhouse and she's smart. You can work with her this summer and when you and Chrissi move to Sioux Falls for the school term, she'll be able to handle the business for you."

Tyler didn't answer.

"It'll be one less thing for you to worry about," Mason pushed.

"You're going to have your hands full," Riley, the father of twin toddlers, added. "You'd be better off to sell."

"I don't know," Tyler finally admitted. "I'll talk with Chris about it."

Erik turned his attention to Matt and his demeanor became more professional. "Everything alright at the paper?" he asked. He was standing, as if ready to leave.

"As far as I know," Matt confirmed. "Davis had threatened to sue, but I don't think he will follow through."

"Did Adam Brewster's mother ever explain why she quit?"

"No. Ashley hasn't heard from her," Matt supplied.

"Has she changed the locks on the building?" Erik grilled.

Matt put his fork down and studied the friend who had transformed into an official in a matter of a few sentences. "Should she?" he asked as a tingle of anxiety inched along his spine.

"I told her to," the other man replied. A frown creased the lawman's features as he added, "I'm guessing she hasn't complied."

Matt shook his head.

"Brewster – the kid – worries me," the sheriff warned. Focusing on Riley he added, "Tell your brother to keep an eye on that girl of his, too. Adam has to have figured out that she's the witness who can place him at the newspaper office the night of the break in."

Riley nodded. "He's got her on a short chain already," he confirmed.

"Good." Erik pushed the chair tight against the table. "I'd better get back to work."

The four men met up at Mrs. Holmes' house hours later to assist the woman who had served as a surrogate grandmother with her homecoming. She'd been hospitalized, and then moved to the nursing home for an additional week of recovery. Her physician had finally decided that she could return to her own home, as long as she wouldn't be alone. Chrissi happily offered to live on the main floor of the home, rather than in the apartment, to help assure that Mrs. Holmes would be fine.

Matt had picked up Chrissi's limited belongings from Melanie's apartment and taken them to Mrs. Holmes' place. He'd also busied himself moving his sister's things from the basement apartment to the main floor bedroom in compliance with the agreed-upon instructions from the women.

Riley had been designated to make a grocery run to restock the perishable food items which had expired while no one was living in the spacious Victorian home. Meanwhile Tyler and Mason trekked to the nursing home to "spring" Mrs. Holmes from the dreaded clutches of the medical community and return her to her beloved home.

As Mrs. Holmes settled in an antique cushioned chair she reached for the hand of the nearest of the men. "Thank you, boys," she said with a wide smile. Her silver eyes danced with merriment as she reached for another hand. "It's so good to be home again."

Matt dropped a kiss on her wrinkled cheek before telling her he'd stop by the next day to see if she needed anything. Riley, glancing to the clock, followed suit saying that he needed to get back to work.

"Come closer," the matriarchal woman commanded with gentle forcefulness, as she shifted her silver gaze to the young lawyer. "So you've become good friends with my boys?" she queried.

Mason had become friends with Andrew while the two attended college, and a few years ago he moved to Miller's Bend and began working in partnership with an old attorney. Mr. Parrsons had died last year, leaving Mason without a partner. Through his friendship with Andrew, Mason had become acquainted with Riley, and then with Riley's friends, Tyler and Matt. He'd gotten to know their wives as each had become a resident of the small town as well.

Mason's ties to the group of friends had deepened and he did, indeed, feel that he was one of them. "Yes, ma'am," he answered. "We've been getting along splendidly," he added, letting some of his inborn Southern charm slip into his mannerisms. He politely kissed the back of her hand and added, "Glad to be of assistance in returning you to your exquisite home."

Mason released the old woman's hand, but her grip on his hand tightened with surprising strength. "Thank you, Mr. Alexander," she commented crisply. "How's the practice going?"

"Just fine."

"Oh, that's too bad," she commented. And then in response to his bewildered expression, she added, "I was hoping it was fantastic. We want to keep our young professionals adequately employed."

"I'm as busy as I can bear alone, Mrs. Holmes," he replied. "Besides, new work for me would mean there is an increase in the nasty side of society," he added with a smile. "We wouldn't want that." He was referring to the workload generated by the fact that he held the position of State's Attorney.

"I trust you're taking care of yourself," she continued.

"I run five miles a day, eat right and only see a doctor when absolutely necessary," he joked.

She laughed at that. "Well that's good," she finally added. "Mind you don't neglect your faith." Mrs. Holmes had released his hand and Mason took advantage of the opportunity to retreat a step.

He believed in God, but didn't go all-out to show his faith to the world. "Well," he suggested after a moment of thought, "You do see me in church nearly every Sunday."

The silvery-gray eyes of the woman seated before Mason, searched his features with a scrutiny that made him uneasy. Finally Mrs. Holmes cocked her head slightly and asked, "Do you suppose that will nearly keep you from the fires of hell?"

The color rose in his cheeks and Mason stammered for an answer. He was educated and seasoned in the art of debate, routinely winning the verbal jousting matches in the courtrooms, and this fragile old woman always seemed able to keep him off-balance with her observations. "I ... I ..." He took a breath and refocused. "Don't you think that's a bit extreme?" he suggested.

"Oh, certainly," she returned. "I only meant to make you think. A rhetorical question if you will." She was smiling and relaxed again, leaning back in the chair. "Take it from me, there are things in this life that you need to have in proper order in order to make it into the next. Do not ignore your faith. You may meet an adversary who makes you question your beliefs ... And the stronger you are, the easier it will be for you to stand your ground."

Somewhat bewildered, Mason assured Mrs. Holmes that he hadn't been bested to date. He promised to heed her advice. Claiming that he needed to get back to the office, he bid her a good day, and left.

He passed Tyler in the kitchen as he was leaving and Tyler was returning from some unknown mission outdoors. "She keeps you on your toes, doesn't she?" Mason noted with a gesture toward the woman ensconced in the living room.

"That she does," Tyler's reply was warm as his focus followed the path indicated by his friend. "That she does." Looking into Mason's face, he asked in a stage whisper, "Has she tried to find you a woman yet?"

An expression of incredulity crossed Mason's face before he shook his head. "No. Is that what happened to you and Chrissi?"

"Not me," Tyler denied. "But I think she pushed Riley and Shelby toward each other; and she had a hand in helping Allison realize she could trust Andrew. She might even have played a role with Matt and Ashley."

Mason whistled low in appreciation. "Finding women for those dogs must have been a challenge, all right," he joked.

"You'd best watch out," Tyler advised. "If she figures she's found the right one for you, you'll be hitched up before you know what hit you." He clapped a hand to Mason's shoulder and laughed in response to the lawyer's stricken look.

"See you around," was the only response Mason gave as he left the house.

"Tyler?" Mrs. Holmes' voice called from the other room.

"Yes, ma'am," he replied as he stepped through the doorway.

"Would you be a dear and bring my blue blanket from my bedroom closet. The fuzzy one," she specified. Then laughing she added, "Fuzzy blanket – not the fuzzy closet."

When he returned with the requested blanket, he unfolded it and spread it over her knees. "What else do you need?" he asked.

"Oh, just visit with me a while," she smiled sweetly.

"I checked the gauge on your fuel," he said as he slipped out of his jacket and settled on the couch across from Mrs. Holmes. "You should be fine for a couple weeks yet. Do you want me to call and order a little more, or do you think it will be warm enough to get by after that?"

She seemed to consider the question before responding, "Please call and have them fill the tank."

"You won't need that much," he began to counter, but Mrs. Holmes stopped him by holding up her right hand.

"I don't want to have to think about it again," she explained. "Just have them fill it, please."

"Yes, ma'am." Mrs. Holmes seemed to be tiring, and she looked uncomfortable. "Maybe I should go ..." he offered, although he really didn't need to leave and he wanted to be near the woman that he hadn't known was his own grandmother until recently.

"No!" she answered quickly. "I'd like to visit with you more. We have important business to discuss." She paused as if considering whether to say the next item on her mind, and then sighed. "Can you do a favor for this old girl?" she asked sweetly.

"I'll try."

Tears stood in her eyes as she quietly formed the question, "Would it be too much to ask you to call me 'Grandma'?"

Tyler's throat tightened and he moved to sit on an ottoman which had been a staple in the living room since for more years than he'd been visiting Mrs. Holmes. He pulled the seat closer to hers and took her hand. "I'd be honored to – I just didn't know if you wanted that."

"I do," she replied. "If you and your father are alright with letting the world – or at least Miller's Bend – know that you're of my family."

Tyler and Jeff had discussed that very question one evening, and Jeff had given his blessing to acknowledging the truth of the relationship, at least amongst their friends. They both knew that the information would travel through the grapevine, but any discomfort caused by that would be well worth counting Mrs. Holmes as a family member. Jeff hadn't disclosed the reasons he and his wife had agreed to keep the secret, saying that story belonged to Mrs. Holmes and it would be up to her to tell it.

"Dad said …" Tyler's voice trailed away and his focus dropped to his hands. He didn't want to go into a lengthy discussion of what his father had said. "He and I want to consider you part of our family if you'd like," he related to her.

Smiling and nodding, Mrs. Holmes answered, "Very much." She sniffled, and repeated, "I'd like it very much."

And just as Tyler opened his mouth to begin asking questions about the past, Mrs. Holmes blindsided him with one of her own, "And now what's this I hear about you and Chrissi Gibson?"

Tyler paused while he considered what his grandmother would want to know. "What do you mean?" he asked as he stalled for time.

"I mean I hear very well for an old lady," she laughed at his surprise. "Tell me about Chrissi. You're a couple?" she demanded gently.

He couldn't keep the smile from his voice, much less try to hide it from his expression. "She's … She's something special," he finally summarized.

"So at last you've realized that you love her?" the wise old woman asked kindly. "Don't look so surprised, young man. I may seem pragmatic, but I assure you, I am a romantic at heart," she continued.

"I wish it was a simple matter of romance," he replied without intending to speak so openly.

Mrs. Holmes – Grandma – swept a hand through the air between them in a dismissive motion. "It is that simple. You are a good man and she's a good woman. Luckily each of you has loved the other for as long as I've been aware," she began. The dismayed expression on her grandson's face stopped her words. "What's the problem?"

A dark look passed over Tyler before he responded. His silver eyes met his grandmother's and he wondered how everyone in town had overlooked the similarity between them. Why had no one ever questioned whether there was a genetic link between them? Thinking again of Chrissi and the issues they would face, the words slipped from his lips on a sigh, "There are ... entailments – complications."

"Complications?" Grandma echoed. "Sounds ominous," she added in an artificially deep and quavering voice. "Shall I sound the alarms?"

"No need for that," he answered as his focus was once again snared in hers.

The bony hand grasped his tightly as she tried to make Tyler understand her next words: "For those who love God, all things work together for good," she quoted from the Bible. "For those who are called according to His purpose."

"What?"

"Look for the good, Tyler," she commanded. "Do not focus your energies on doubts or misgivings. If you trust in your heart that God approves of your union, then trust in Him to see you through the complications as well."

"Sounds good," he admitted. "But -"

"No buts!" his grandmother counseled. "You don't trust in the Lord part way. Either you trust in Him or you don't."

"You know I do." Doubt still danced in the shadows behind Tyler's eyes. He'd been being the self-assured one; bolstering Chrissi when she had hesitated; convincing her family that they truly love each other, and shouldering the blame for the pregnancy. He'd been afraid to allow even a sliver of uncertainty to enter his bearing in front of anyone. Until today; until the depth of his friendship with Mrs. Holmes allowed him to let down his guard.

"Oh, my," she whispered at reading his trepidation. "It's that serious?"

"Yes," he confirmed. "It's that serious."

"You need to marry the girl," the old woman observed with an annoying confidence.

Tyler bristled slightly. "I don't *need* to marry her," he attested, as he wondered which of his friends had brought Mrs. Holmes up to speed on the situation. "I *want* to marry her."

"Hmm," was the response. "You can have the ceremony here if you'd like."

"You approve?"

"It isn't mine to approve or disapprove," his grandmother said philosophically. "Just as it isn't the place of any other soul in this town to judge your relationship."

When Tyler's skin flushed and he looked as if he was about to reveal too much information, Mrs. Holmes stopped him. "You truly love her. I know you have for a long time," she looked away as if recalling past events. "You used to carry her on your back when she tried to tag along with you boys and would surely have fallen behind. I swear, Matt would have tied her to a tree and left her behind, but you wouldn't have stood for that." Her gaze returned to Tyler's as she spoke, "It was a different kind of love back then, to be sure. But you've always cared for that girl."

"Our ages -"

"The difference isn't really that great," she appeased his concern. "Not in the scope of things and certainly not if you take a historical view."

A crooked smile lifted one side of Tyler's mouth. "You make it sound so easy."

"It can be so easy," she counseled. "Trust your heart and trust in the Lord. Let yourselves love each other and take care of each other. The rest will fall into place."

Tyler's confidence was returning. "Thank you - for the advice. And thank you for offering us the use of your home. I'll check with Chrissi and see how she feels about having the ceremony here."

"You are very welcome," his grandmother replied warmly. And then changing subjects she asked, "Have you started reading the book yet?"

Tyler shook his head. "Sorry. I haven't had a chance."

"You might want to make time for it," she answered. He responded that he would try, and said his good-byes. He strode to his pickup with a whirlpool of ideas in his head, and increasing confidence and love in his heart.

Cadee Brystal

CHAPTER FIFTEEN

There are moments when a person realizes with painful clarity that they should have heeded the advice which they'd chosen to disregard. Ashley was experiencing one of those moments – she should have changed the locks on the doors at the office. Surprise was only the first of the emotions that ricocheted through her as she surveyed the damage to the Chronicle office.

When she arrived at work, the front door of the building had been propped open using the remains of a splintered antique clock from the back room. Without touching the door or its frame, she peeked through the open space into the lobby and discovered more destruction. Ashley had stepped back, leaning against the pillar in front of the building and numbly dialed Sheriff Dunn's cell.

She called Shelby and Tim, the newspaper's graphic artist, telling them there was no need to come to work for the next few hours. Shelby, of course, wouldn't leave her friend to deal with the new catastrophe on her own and rushed to the office, arriving as Ashley was disconnecting the call she'd made to let Matt know what had happened. Erik Dunn and Jeff Schuster were both inside the building by then, making a preliminary walk-through, and deputies and police officers seemed to swarm the area.

"At least this week's paper is out," Shelby offered as a weak sort of consolation as she wrapped her friend in a warming embrace.

Schuster and Dunn appeared beside the women, having made their initial pass through the interior of the building. The police chief whistled low before adding, "Somebody went to a lot of trouble in there." He looked from Ashley to Shelby and back, taking in their shocked expressions. "I think we'd better get you two down to the station until we can get a better handle on what's happened in there," he said indicating the office of the Chronicle with a sweep of his hand.

Ashley shook her head defiantly. "It's my business. I can't just go sit somewhere and wait," she argued as her husband's car screeched to a stop adjacent to the building. Her heart fluttered with relief as he hurried to her side.

Matt's strong arms pulled Ashley close to his chest and she felt his heart racing. The tender moment passed quickly, when Matt's gaze drilled the police chief, demanding answers. "What happened here? Who is doing this to Ashley?"

"We'll get to the bottom of this, Matt," Jeff answered calmly. "Can you just take the ladies somewhere else for a while and let us work?"

Ashley's eyes lit with indignant irritation and she raised her chin before responding, "I will not be taken somewhere! This is my business and I need to start putting things right. We've got work to do, too."

The chief shook his head in sad commiseration. "You won't be doing anything in there today. And tomorrow you probably can't do much other than cleaning up," he said. "And you'll need to order new computers. Whoever did this smashed every computer and printer in the place. Go home and wait; go to the police station; go to Matt's studio, or go shopping. But you are not going to be able to set foot in there for hours – not until we collect every scrap of evidence we possibly can."

Hours later, the trio joined Riley for lunch in his office at the metal fabrication plant. The women had spent a great deal of time writing up every strange or damaging incident that had occurred over the preceding months. Shortly after the change of ownership there had been problems: money missing from the till, the disastrous issue in which someone had flooded the front page with typos and moved the stories randomly about, lost digital files and the furnace in the basement of the old building had been vandalized. They'd assumed that the man who had been employed as the reporter at the time, Neal, was to blame because he had openly disliked Ashley. They'd assumed it was an attempt to drive her away.

Once the police had questioned Neal, he had resigned and left town. The problems had ceased, and Ashley had convinced Shelby to return to work at the newspaper. "I never understood why Neal would have done those things," Riley said before biting into his pizza.

"To try to scare Ashley?" Shelby suggested.

"But she'd already purchased the business. What good would it do to scare her?" he countered. "She wasn't going to leave."

Ashley interjected, "He had told me that he planned to be the editor – maybe he had designs on ownership?"

"Why not just offer to buy you out if that was the case?" Riley asked. "And if he wanted to own it, why would he cause the kind of damage that he did?"

"I don't think we'll figure out why Neal did the things he did," Shelby offered. "We need to focus on what's happening now."

"The chief asked us to include all those older incidents for him, too. Maybe it is all related," Ashley countered.

"Why would anybody want to damage the newspaper?" Matt asked. "I mean, everyone benefits from having a local business that's embedded in the community. And this is a really good newspaper."

"You're biased, honey," Ashley answered sweetly before rewarding him with a quick kiss.

"No, he's right," Shelby said. "It is a very good newspaper and it's getting better under your guidance. Maybe the competition can't take it."

"So … you're saying what? The daily newspaper from 50 miles away is so scared of us that they sent thugs over to smash our computers?" Ashley laughed at the idea. "Not likely!"

"No. Probably not." Shelby snatched a second slice of pizza.

"So we ruled out professional jealousy," Riley concluded.

"What about someone who is angry about your reporting?" Matt suggested. "Remember, Shelby had Mr. Jones angry enough to blow his top in public meetings a couple of years ago. Maybe you two have irritated someone else who is powerful, but better at hiding his anger?"

Riley's gaze sliced to his wife, "Shel, honey, are you working on any exposing fraud and corruption again?"

Her eyes rounded in an exaggerated expression of innocence and her hand fluttered to her chest. "Who? Little ol' me? Why – I wouldn't dream of such a thing!" she declared sweetly.

Riley rolled his eyes. "Of course not," he said flatly. "Ash, you might want to fire her before she gets your building burned to the ground. We'd hate lose the oldest brick building in the county."

"You can't burn brick," Shelby argued.

Steven, one of Riley's employees entered the office. "Sorry to interrupt," he said. "I need to get a copy of the order for the McKlintlock project." Riley nodded and gestured toward the file cabinet, indicating that Steven should help himself.

Matt picked up the conversational flow. "Wait a minute," he said as he turned an accusing look toward his wife. "You said the guy at the cheese plant threatened to sue you a couple weeks ago …"

"So?" Ashley asked hesitantly. "He isn't going to sue. He doesn't have a leg to stand on."

"How can you be so sure?" Matt argued.

"Mason reviewed Shelby's notes and the recording of her interviews. He said we had nothing to worry about …" Ashley's voice trailed away as her focus flew to Shelby's. Alarm flared in their expressions as they simultaneously reached the same conclusion.

Shelby finished the sentence, "… as long as my notes and recording are kept in a safe place! That's what this break-in was about! He was after my notes."

"We don't know that," Riley said soothingly.

"Besides," Matt added, "Davis isn't the kind of man who's going to do physical damage to the building. He wouldn't want to break a sweat."

"But he's got friends," Shelby suggested. "And they've got friends."

"And he's got money," Riley added. "He could hire the dirty work done, if he wanted to intimidate you."

They were silent a moment as each let the idea slip around in his or her mind, considering whether this was a plausible theory.

"Uh, boss?" Steven asked as if he was afraid of breaking the silence. The man had worked at the business even before Riley had purchased it, and he'd grown to respect Riley. But in truth, Steven had a soft spot in his heart for Riley's wife. And now he looked to Shelby as he spoke, "I've seen him – Ethan Davis – down at the Outlaw Bar in Montevideo. He ain't as uppity as you think he is. He just gets out of town when he wants to … play."

The energy in the room pulsed and everyone seemed to hold their breath as they waited for more.

"And?" Shelby prompted softly.

Steven's gaze darted around the room as if he wished he hadn't started this conversation at all. He glanced at the open doorway as if contemplating making a break for it. But then his gaze came back to Shelby's face. "And," he croaked. "And he sometimes has Warren with him."

Blank stares answered his statement, as if they didn't understand.

"Warren?" Shelby whispered. "Warren, who?"

Steven's voice was gruff when he replied, "Warren … Brewer." The big man disappeared through to doorway before anyone spoke.

The implications settled for a moment. Could it be possible that the rumored friendship between Ethan Davis, a man who wanted to sue Ashley and the Chronicle, and Warren Brewer, Adam's father, and Bobbie's ex-husband, could be the missing link to the strange things that had been happening at the newspaper?

"Call Jeff," Matt ordered in a voice rougher than usual. "They need to check on this."

"Take me back to the office," Shelby issued an order of her own. "I need to check on my notes and recordings ... If they got those, we could be in trouble. Then it's his word against mine." Her gaze met Ashley's, "I'm sorry."

The women rose and grabbed their bags, but Riley stopped them. A scowl creased his forehead as he spoke, "Hold up. That doesn't make sense."

"What?" the women answered in unison.

"There was trouble before you did any stories about the cheese plant expansion," he said thoughtfully. "That can't be at the heart of the problems."

"You think they are unrelated?" Ashley asked. "You mean we have two people attacking the paper?"

"Could be," Riley answered with a shrug. "It just doesn't make sense when you try to push the first incidents together with the recent break-ins, especially if you try to tie it all to the stories about the cheese plant."

"Maybe it's not about the paper at all," Shelby suggested as her expression changed to one of fear. "What if it's personal? What if someone is trying to get to you, Ashley?"

By the end of the work day, the women had shared their theories with the police chief and the sheriff, and Ashley had placed an order for new computers. The new state-of-the-art equipment would arrive Friday, along with a technician to get everything set up and transfer data from the damaged machines to the new ones. With luck they would put out the next issue, although it was likely to be small, on time. They'd been relieved to find that Shelby's notes had remained safely locked away in the antique safe – the one with eight-inch-thick walls and two sets of doors requiring not only a combination to be opened, but also a key. It was a good safe.

Ashley also made arrangements to have the locks on the building replaced the following day. If anyone was going to trash her business, they were going to have to actually break in the next time. Those old keys floating around town would not work in her doors by this time tomorrow.

CHAPTER SIXTEEN

Rori supposed things could be worse. Maybe.

She was feeling a little like Cinderella ... not during the royal ball, instead during the time of her life when she served the household as if she were an indentured servant. Washing and scrubbing and doing her parents' bidding. She'd been stripped of her privileges, including friends, cell phone, iPod and computer – unless it was for homework. And if she did need to use the computer, she had to stay in the presence of one of her parents.

She was grounded and being punished. Under the current edict from her father and step-mother, Rori was allowed to be one of exactly four places: school, home, church, or en route from the high school to pick up her sister, Hope, from the afterschool program and see her safely home. And she had been assigned extra chores at home ... work, work, work. As if that would help her see the error of being affiliated with Adam Brewer.

Mercifully, Andrew and Allison hadn't focused on the fact that Rori had been riding around with a 20-year-old man. That fact seemed to pale in comparison to Sheriff Dunn's assertion that since Brewer had been charged with one break-in at the Chronicle, she had become an accessory in the commission of felony burglary. Chrissi had been right – Adam was trouble – Rori conceded as she trudged down the splintered sidewalk that edged a quiet residential street.

Chrissi's words came back to her as she walked: If you think you're old enough to make your own decisions, at least make intelligent ones. As much as she hated to agree with anyone just now, Rori had to admit that Chrissi's advice had been sound. Rori certainly hadn't proven that she could handle herself by blowing off her responsibilities and riding around with Adam.

The two were half-way home, Rori ambling along, lost in her thoughts, and Hope scampering beside her and chattering loudly. The school day had been stressful with numerous tests and quizzes and tons of homework. Oh yeah, and Mrs. Buckley had flipped out on Rori, and given her extra homework … like she needed that. The breeze picked up a little, and Rori sensed something riding on its currents – whether a noise or a scent – it grabbed her attention. Instinctively, she grabbed Hope's hand and started moving faster toward home. In the same second, she turned her head to look behind, just as Adam's fingers tangled in her dark shoulder-length hair.

Rori's scalp burned as he snagged her and, using the grip in her tresses, wrenched her back so she landed hard on the ground at his feet. Gone was the smiling, cajoling, handsome older man she'd spent several afternoons riding around with in his hot pickup. Gone was her naïve belief that she could handle herself. Gone were her feelings that her parents were paranoid and overprotective.

He quickly yanked Rori's slight body back to her feet, and with anger glittering in his eyes he spoke with anger. "You little witch!" he yelled so close to her face that she felt the revolting pinpricks of his spittle hitting her forehead. His breath carried the bitter scent of alcohol, like her birth mother's used to, and Rori's stomach clenched. "You told the cops I was the one who broke into the Chronicle." Rori moved to wipe the offensive substance from her face, but he blocked her movement, capturing her wrist in a vise-like grip.

She slashed at his face with her free hand, her fingernails leaving a bloodied trail on his cheek. Cold malice contorted Adam's face as he spoke again. "You're coming with me," he laughed as he yanked hard on her hair, jerking Rori back the way they'd come.

Trying to twist away, Rori noted that Hope had run for safety, as her sister had taught her to do. The little girl was pounding on the door of Mrs. Fields' house. A faint ripple of relief swept over Rori as she realized that at least Hope would be safe. Rori's mind flashed to the time, before her father had married Allison, when Rori's own mother and another man had kidnapped her and Hope. She'd been younger then, more than two years younger, and hadn't known how to fight off two adults, and keep Hope safe at the same time. But this was different.

An instinct Rori didn't know she had kicked in and she pulled back. Renewed pain shot through her scalp and neck as she heaved against Adam's attempts to drag her toward his waiting truck. Her fear turned to anger when he spoke again. "You are a little hellion, aren't you? Go ahead and fight me – I'll teach you a lesson you won't forget."

Instead of continuing to pull, Rori lurched forward, ramming into Adam's tall form, pushing him off balance. His foot caught on an edge of concrete that protruded sharply in the sidewalk. The combination of his drunkenness and his surprise at being pushed off-balance by the girl's attack, gave Rori a few seconds to run away as his arms flailed wildly. She'd only gone a few strides however, when his body hit hers from behind, slamming her to the ground.

Pain streaked through her wrist as she tried to scramble away from his prone body. His drunkenness was working for Rori and she tried to dash toward the safety of Mrs. Fields' home before he could nab her again. Adam tackled her again, and this time she wasn't so lucky. He'd wrapped his arms around her as they fell toward the still-frozen turf and she landed hard on her side, with his much heavier frame pinning her there. Her hands remained shackled uselessly by her sides as she struggled. His demeanor had changed again, as Adam spoke quietly now. "My sweet Aurora, you know you're meant for me … I've invested so much time and energy -"

Rori hadn't seen what happened as she'd lain beneath his bulk, battling for freedom, but she'd heard a sound, and then Adam's words had stopped abruptly. His body had gone limp and fallen away from her.

A new voice sounded, close to her face. "Rori? Oh, No! Rori!"

She recognized the voice, but through the haze of pain and fear, her mind was having trouble naming its owner. Involuntarily, her muscle strained to push away from the inert form beside her even while gentle hands touched her shoulder and brushed her hair away from her face. "Stay still, Rori. He's not going to hurt you," the voice repeated. "You're safe. Stay still. You're safe."

She heard a softness in the voice that soothed her, but it wasn't until she focused on Adam's still body, that she let herself believe she was safe from him. Closing her eyes, she asked on a whisper, "Is Hope safe?"

"She's safe," came the answer. "She's with my grandma." And then Rori knew whose hands touched her so carefully, whose voice had calmed her, whose character had driven him to step into danger's path to save her from Adam. Daniel. Daniel Fields.

The last thought Rori had before she passed out was that she was the biggest idiot in the Miller's Bend School.

Voices interrupted Rori's dream – harsh, angry voices. Her mind was muddled … like when a person is just waking up. And then she realized that she was just waking up, but she couldn't quite get there. She tried to focus on the voices, but the sound was usually muted garble, with an occasional interjection of loud clear words. She recognized that voice readily enough and sighed with contentment. It was her dad's voice.

Dad was here … he would protect her.

Protect her? From … what? Rori struggled to bring her thoughts into focus. Finally, having gained no headway in her mind, she forced her eyes open the tiniest of degrees. She saw Hope leaning against her mother's shoulder as the two looked through a picture book. Rori always felt a little guilty that she had benefited so much when her father had married Allison, bringing her a mother and sister who loved her. But why were they sitting in Rori's room watching her sleep? And why was Dad so upset?

Rori's eyes fluttered closed again, and Hope must have noticed because in that second, she scrambled off her mother's lap and quickly crossed to Rori's side. "I think she's awake, Mama," Hope's sweet voice sounded.

"Don't touch her, honey," came Allison's reply. "Remember she has bruises all over, okay?" Rori drifted back to sleep.

When she awoke again, her parents both nested in nearby chairs, and Hope slept crosswise at the foot of her bed. "Dad?" she croaked.

Worry marred the handsome face of her father as he appeared at her bedside. "Hey, honey. How ya' feeling?" He lightly skimmed her right arm, until he reached her hand which he clasped gently. "Do you have pain?"

She hadn't thought that far, and moved the shake her head in a negative response, but agony shot through her neck, radiating up the back of her skull and down into her shoulders simultaneously. She gasped in response, which caused a jagged torment in her midsection. When she would have pulled her right hand to her mouth to stifle a cry, her father caught the limb, saving Rori from thumping her face with a cast.

She concentrated on breathing. Inhaling deeply hurt Rori's ribs, she discovered after one attempt. She settled for shallow breaths.

Rori was released from the hospital the morning after … She didn't really want to think on it too much. She'd been interviewed by Tyler's dad, the police chief whom she'd thought was still on leave after he'd been shot. Apparently he'd returned to active duty sometime without her realizing it. When Chief Schuster talked with her, he used the word attack. It was a nice word, she thought.

Rori had also heard her father talking with the chief, and with his friend Mason, who was a lawyer. When the men talked they used other words: attempted kidnapping, attempted rape, and attempted murder. They didn't know she'd heard these things, but Rori shivered every time she repeated them in her mind.

What would have happened if Daniel hadn't stepped in? Fear wrapped its icy fingers around her heart when she considered the question. Her body was healing, but her spirit was faltering. What would have happened? Why did this happen? How could something good come from her experience?

A soft knock on Rori's bedroom door interrupted her dismal questions. She'd been at home for two days, with nothing to do but think while she rested and her body mended. Allison was wonderful to her and Hope was a joy, but Rori couldn't really relate everything that was on her mind to either of them. Her dad loved her deeply and spent much time with her, but if she broached the story of what had happened, she would see anger in his eyes and he wouldn't speak of it.

"Come in," she called in response to the knock.

There was a second of hesitation before it opened, and Chrissi peeked past the wooden panel. She smiled broadly as she stepped inside the sun-filled room. "The things a girl will do to get out of gym class for a few days ..." Chrissi joked as she approached the bed where Rori sat, propped up on a backdrop of pillows. "Are you in solitary confinement?" she added as she glanced around the room.

Rori automatically reached out to hug her friend as Chrissi approached. The twinge in her midsection reminded her of the injuries to her ribs. "I'm taking a break from Mom," Rori replied with a smile. "She's been fussing over me too much." Chrissi remembered how quickly Rori and her stepmother had bonded. With the girl's birth mother gone, Rori had no compulsions about letting Allison be "Mom" to her. They were lucky to have each other.

"What's been going on at school?" Rori inquired as she scooted toward the headboard and pulled her legs up, making space for Chrissi to join her on the bed. The older girl took a similar position near the foot of the bed and deluged Rori with all the news of the high school social scene.

When the conversation wound down of its own accord, Chrissi leaned closer to Rori. "I want to ask an important favor of you," she began. Apprehension gripped Rori as she took in the seriousness in her friend's expression. Ever since she'd known Chrissi, Rori had looked up to her as a role model. And since their families spent much time together, there had been points in their lives when they'd felt like cousins, or even sisters.

"Anything," Rori replied quickly, even without hearing the request. "What do you need?" she asked with wide-eyed anticipation.

"A maid of honor." The excitement she felt surprised even Chrissi as she spoke the words. "I'm getting married!" Chrissi realized that she was genuinely happy about the impending marriage. Joy danced in her eyes and radiated from her as she made the announcement; her cheeks flushed with vibrancy.

"Right," Rori responded. "You have prom next week and finals in two more weeks. Then there's graduation. You can't get married – you won't have time," she added with light-spirited sarcasm. "So the wedding is when? In three years? Maybe four?"

The mention of school seemed to deflate Chrissi a little. "More like next month," she informed in all seriousness.

"Next month?!" Disbelief painted Rori's features. "You can't be serious!"

"I am serious," Chrissi asserted. Realizing that she'd left out an important component of the equation. "Tyler and I are getting married right after graduation. And I'd be honored -"

"Tyler?!" Rori screeched as she hurtled off the bed. The sudden movement had pain rippling around her ribcage again, but Rori ignored it. She squinted at Chrissi as if trying to divine the truth. "Tyler, who?" she asked cautiously.

A deep blush burned Chrissi's cheeks and she lifted her chin as she rose to face her friend. "Tyler Schuster," she defined clearly.

"He's old!" the younger girl pointed out unnecessarily.

"Well … maybe to you -"

"Maybe?" Rori asked. "He's got to be like 40!"

"No, he's not," Chrissi countered while executing an exaggerated an eye roll.

The adolescent impertinence washed over Rori as she did some quick math. She stood tall and conceded, "Okay. He's not 40. But I'd bet your college fund he's over 25."

Chrissi nodded, understanding where Rori was headed with the conversation. "Yes, he is over 25. And I'm over 18 – an adult. You are a sophomore in high school."

"You're a hypocrite." Rori turned her back and feigned intense interest in the books that lined a shelf over her desk.

Chrissi eased closer and touched her friend's shoulder. "I'm not being hypocritical," she said.

"You are too!" Rori hissed. "I'll bet there are twice as many years between you and Tyler, than between me and Adam," Rori pressed.

"You're a minor; Adam's 20," Chrissi argued. "That makes it wrong for him to date you. Besides – he's a criminal!"

Rori growled as her surprise emerged as anger. She didn't understand why she was arguing the point, since she'd decided for herself that Adam was trouble and she had no interest in spending more time with him. And that was before he'd tackled her and tried to drag her into his truck. But for some reason she couldn't stop herself from the amplifying the dispute. "Is this an intelligent decision?" she asked hotly, referring to Chrissi's advice weeks earlier.

"Yes," Chrissi replied without pause. "Yes it is. And I'm lucky that things worked out so Tyler and I would have the chance to reveal our feelings." Rori ignored her. "Look at me," the older girl instructed. "I'm an adult, and even though there's a difference in our ages Tyler and I love each other."

Skepticism shadowed Rori's young eyes. "Really? Chrissi, is it truly love? The kind that lasts – not the kind Lucy thought was right?" she demanded, referring to her birth mother.

Repeating the question in her mind, Chrissi felt her confidence in the relationship grow. "Yes, I'm sure it's truly love – the kind that lasts," she affirmed as tears built in her eyes. "He loves me more than I had imagined."

"How can you know he's the right one for you?" Rori challenged. "You haven't even dated anyone else more than a few times." The younger girl was casting another speculative glance over Chrissi again when she spoke. "For that matter, I didn't even know you had dated Tyler …"

Here we go, Chrissi thought as she subconsciously took a retreating step. "We've known each other a long time." She crossed her arms across her chest and cocked a hip. "We have been hanging out a lot since … lately."

Advancing as if she was a well-trained prosecuting attorney, Rori drilled, "But when did you date? When did he pick you up and take you to dinner? A movie? Is he taking you to the prom?"

Chrissi couldn't answer because they'd never done any of those things. *Lord, how do I answer this?* She closed her eyes and breathed. Rori was a close friend, practically family, and she was at an age where she questioned everything about relationships. The girl's mother could have been a poster child for forming destructive relationships, and Rori had already been exploring the dating field. Her time spent with Adam had, of course, been brief, but would leave a lasting impression.

Would Rori try to emulate Chrissi's relationship with Tyler based on misconceptions? And what would she think when she learned of the pregnancy? Chrissi didn't have the answers.

She tried to shake off the unease the questions stirred in her mind. "Tyler's a good man," Chrissi whispered when she opened her eyes. "He loves me so much that he was prepared to deny his feelings so that I could follow my dreams," she said. "He didn't want to interfere."

"What changed?" Rori asked casually. She crossed her arms and waited for a reply.

Evasively the older of the two replied, "What do you mean?"

Rori's slender eyebrow rose as her expression seemed to ask whether she looked that gullible. "I mean, you said he didn't want to interfere with your dreams," she explained. "Now it would seem that's exactly what's happened. No college for you!"

"He's going to help me," Chrissi countered. "He's going to hire a manager for the business and go with me to Sioux Falls."

"He's not going to help you reach your goals, Chrissi," Rori replied coldly. Turning away, she surveyed the posters that covered her walls to avoid letting her friend see the moisture in her eyes. "He's going to want to come back here – to Miller's Bend – once you've gotten your education. And you're going to want to move on to a large city where you can be a neonatal nurse." After a shaky breath, Rori once again faced Chrissi. "Don't you see?" she beseeched. "He'll help you get your education, but your dream is to *be* a neonatal nurse; not just *train to be* a neonatal nurse. And as soon as he drags you back to this little town, you'll be just a plain old nurse. Not saving babies; not helping new mothers; just monitoring boring stuff and changing bedpans!"

The sting of Rori's words cut deeper than Chrissi had expected and, in all honesty she had already seen the turn in the road ahead. The turn where what she'd believed her destiny to be became invisible, but a new future had opened up in another direction. "Rori," she sighed. "Sometimes a person has to adjust their dreams." She looked out the window. Saw the birds carrying objects to fill their nests. She noted the beautiful early spring flowers – crocus, tulips and daffodils – dancing in the breeze in Andrew's flower beds. Beds designed and planted by Tyler.

The man had an unusual talent for taking a plain piece of nature and turning it into a thing of exceptional beauty. Not every landscaper could perform the transformations that Tyler was able to do. His work brought happiness to everyone who laid eyes on it, and Chrissi filled with pride that she could be associated with him.

"Sometimes our dreams change, Rori," she repeated. "Sometimes they mature into actual attainable goals.

Sometimes you meet someone and you want to find a way to merge your separate, individual goals into shared ones." She sighed before concluding, "Ty loves me. I want to be his wife. We love each other and we want to raise a family together," Chrissi tried to explain. "We are happy about this, and I need you to be happy with me."

When Rori didn't answer, Chrissi pulled her gaze away from the view outside the window to try to gauge her friend's reaction. The disbelief and suspicion she saw in the younger girl's face immobilized her. "Rori?" she whispered.

"Family?!" Rori snarled. The look turned to accusation and anger. "He got you pregnant!" She snapped her mouth closed and turned away. "I'll kill him," she breathed as she headed for the door.

CHAPTER SEVENTEEN

Rori's murderous threat against Tyler was probably a bluff. Probably. But Chrissi couldn't let her leave when she was so upset. And she couldn't let her leave thinking so lowly of him. He hadn't done the things Rori assumed he had. He'd done nothing to deserve the harsh judgment Tyler would take in response to Chrissi's pregnancy.

"No!" Chrissi caught her friend by her cast-free arm and spun her so they were face to face again. "No."

"No?" Rori challenged. "What then?"

Chrissi tried to lighten the mood. "We don't go around killing our best friends' fiancés," she offered.

"We don't go around sleeping with older guys who get us pregnant," Rori countered. Sarcasm laced her following words, "Or do we? Maybe I should bail Adam out of jail and see what happens?"

The taunt hit its mark and Chrissi fought to keep her voice low, "Don't be stupid! Don't you ever put yourself in a position where you can't take care of yourself."

"I thought that if a guy cares for you, then he's supposed to take care of you," Rori accused. "Tyler's really taken care of you, hasn't he?"

Pain sliced through Chrissi and she tightened her grip on Rori's arm. "You don't understand anything," she rasped. "It's not like that." But how could she understand? When they'd decided to hide the truth, they had stripped their friends the means to understand the situation. Hadn't they forced people to assume that they'd gone against their beliefs?

"You can't understand," Chrissi repeated.

"Let go of me." Rori looked pointedly at the hand that gripped her arm. "I understand plenty."

Chrissi forced her hand away from her friend. The need to defend Tyler rose up within her and, before she'd realized the corner she was painting herself into, the words flowed from her lips. "Tyler has done nothing but be loving and supportive," she cried.

"You've been brainwashed," Rori accused. Pointing toward Chrissi's midsection, she added, "That's not what you get from support. That's what you get from fooling around."

"He's never touched me!" Chrissi shouted, and suddenly realized what she'd said. Her eyes grew large in her face, her hand clasped over her mouth and she turned away. *What have I done?*

Adrenaline carried Rori forward. "Oh? What? Now it's immaculate conception?" she hissed. But then she fell silent. Rori's rich dark eyes narrowed to slits as she studied her friend. Chrissi's back was to her and Rori saw her shoulders jump with a silent sob. Suddenly a sense of shame slipped over Rori. Was Chrissi telling the truth about Tyler? If he hadn't … then … someone else …

Rori closed her mind to the thought. It was difficult enough to believe Chrissi would have given herself to a man she knew well and had entertained thoughts of marrying; there was no way she'd have succumbed to the advances of anyone in a more casual setting. A gasp slipped past Rori's lips as the conclusion lodged in her heart. The only way that had happened would have been against Chrissi's will.

"Chrissi?" Rori's voice was small, and she hated the fear she heard in it. "I'm sorry, Chrissi," she whispered. "I didn't mean to make you cry." She laid a trembling hand to her friend's back. "You're telling the truth?"

Chrissi hesitated. If she confirmed that Tyler had done nothing, she opened the door to questions that would reveal the truth. But she doubted that she had the emotional fortitude to look into her friend's face and tell her that Tyler was at the root of her trouble. She didn't respond and apparently Rori took it as confirmation.

"I'm so sorry," the younger girl said as she wrapped Chrissi into a sisterly embrace. "I didn't know ... I swear, I didn't mean any of it."

Chrissi needed to refocus the conversation for fear of breaking down completely. Weakly she whispered, "Tyler's a good man. You can't condemn him for this."

"I won't," Rori interrupted. "I won't ever again." They held each other as their tears ran free and their friendship renewed itself without words. Finally when they'd run dry, Rori voiced one more question: "When is the baby due?"

With a sniffle, Chrissi, answered, "September."

Rori nodded. In her mind she knew that something must have happened while Chrissi had been away. In Chicago. Alone. "You're right," she said, agreeing with her friend's earlier assertion. "Tyler is a good man."

Chrissi drew back and offered her friend a fragile smile. "You can't tell -"

"I can give you my counselor's name," Rori interrupted the statement Chrissi had been about to deliver. She moved to her iPod to retrieve the contact information.

Chrissi shook her head in denial. "That's not necessary."

With an unconvinced glance, Rori copied down the name and phone number and attempted to hand the information to her friend. "Trust me, Dr. Kingston is a great help," she said warmly. "She's helped me with all that stuff a girl goes through when her mother is a misguided druggie who tries to kidnap her and then dies in a fiery car crash." She smiled an ironic smile, but shadows of regret flickered in Rori's eyes. "It takes a few meetings, but she can help you through it."

Chrissi was still shaking her head, or maybe the action had stopped and restarted. "I can't …"

Rori didn't seem to notice. "Dad and I counseled with Pastor Mark, too," she offered helpfully.

"No!" Chrissi's voice was high and the word scraped at the back of her throat. "*Nobody* here can know about this!" And in a statement that could have been comical if the topic hadn't been so serious she added, "*You* can't even know about this."

"You can't hide it away, Chrissi," Rori countered. "It's not healthy."

The girl even sounded like a therapist.

"You're going to need help. You and Tyler both," Rori suggested. "He's going to need to know what you've been through."

"No. He can't." Chrissi's words were cold. "I can't have him thinking of … that … when he looks at me."

Sincere concern stood in Rori's expression and Chrissi marveled that the girl could vacillate between a broody, petulant teen and a mature, loving woman so quickly. "You are getting married, Chrissi," Rori said slowly. She drew out and carefully enunciated the final word for extra impact.

Not keeping up, Chrissi nodded numbly.

Rori rolled her eyes and blew a stray lock of hair away from her face. "You're going to have to – you know ..." She shrugged with embarrassment. "Is that going to work for you?" she asked with heartfelt emotion. "I mean ... what if you freak out or something?"

These were questions she'd pushed back into the quiet corners of her mind, preferring not to worry about them. But thanks to her friend, Chrissi had to let her internal concerns about intimacy resurface. She flushed as her senses remembered the tenderness in Tyler's hands as he'd held her during recent weeks. Even when they'd kissed, she'd felt nothing but love and excitement and exhilaration. He hadn't – not once – frightened her in anyway.

"I ... I think it will be okay," she whispered.

Rori's analytical mind was working quickly. "But what if something reminds you of ... when it happened? What if you panic?" Innocent eyes search Chrissi's face before she whispered, "How do you not think of it all the time?"

Chrissi's gaze dropped to the floor. "I don't have any memory of it."

"You don't ..."

As if in a trance, Chrissi outlined what had happened to her. While in Chicago attempting to save her cousin, Maddy, she'd been held captive by a drug dealer ... the man who Maddy was tangled up with. She'd been locked in a bare room for days, shackled to the wall and guarded. Four different men worked as guards and one of them had been kind – the one who turned out to be an undercover special agent, Joseph Stockard. After relieving another guard, he had noticed that Chrissi seemed to have been drugged. And she'd had horrifying nightmares. Stockard had deduced that one of the guards had given her Rohypnol or a similar drug and raped her. The agent had tried to protect her for the duration of her captivity.

"He even came here with me to be sure I got home alright because they hadn't captured the man who … assaulted me – during the raid," she concluded.

Rori's eyes rounded as she grasped the story. "So the gunman – the one who came here, to Miller's Bend, and killed Agent Stockard and shot Tyler's dad – he's the one who …?" She shivered involuntarily. "Does Tyler know this? Any of it?"

Chrissi's shoulders rose in a defeated shrug. "Some. Not details."

"He needs to know," Rori asserted. "You have to give him a chance to work through his reactions, too. It's only fair." She pushed the paper with Dr. Kingston's contact information into Chrissi's pocket.

"You said that Tyler's been loving and supportive," the younger girls said slowly. When Chrissi nodded and smiled, Rori continued, "He's going to need some of that love and support back from you sometimes, you know."

Chrissi's brow creased as she considered the advice of her much-wiser-than-her-years friend. "I hadn't thought of it that way, but I suppose you're right," she conceded.

Worry was clearly written on Rori's features when she replied, "I was six when Dad - Andrew - married my mother. And even as young as I was, I knew it wasn't right. Looking at him together with Allison now, I see how a marriage can be." Rori grasped Chrissi's shoulders as if she wished to shake her friend. "Now that I have their relationship to compare it to, I know that my mother never reciprocated Andrew's emotions. She acted trapped."

"Andrew's not your father?" Chrissi asked as if she wasn't following the story. "I never knew that ... you seem so close ..."

"We are close," Rori affirmed. "When they got married, he adopted me – so he is my dad." Her gaze held Chrissi's as she continued, "Andrew is the only father I've known, he just wasn't there when I was conceived."

"Dad and I love each other and he did love my mom – or at least he tried to, but she couldn't love him back." The girl's expression darkened as she recalled some formerly tucked away memories. "It got really ugly. She grew to hate him." Rori's eyes filled with tears again, "She grew to hate me."

Chrissi blinked against the scenes Rori's words painted and winced away from the implications. "You mean I'd be better off alone?"

"No." Rori swiped tears away from her cheeks in a self-conscious move. "I'm saying that it won't work if it's a one-sided relationship. Tyler might be a good man. He might love you enough to try to build a relationship with you and a baby that's not his, but he's not strong enough to succeed unless you are willing and able to meet him halfway. You have to go into this marriage looking at what you can do to reciprocate."

"I don't understand?"

"I don't know how else to say it ... you have to love him back," Rori advised. "Make him your partner, not your safety net. Commit to him; commit to the relationship."

"How did you get so smart?" Chrissi asked.

Rori's smile broke across her face, and she answered, "You really don't want to know."

"I'm so lucky to have you as a best friend," Chrissi said. "What would I do without you?"

"There's just no telling," Rori answered. And then she smiled with wisdom beyond her adolescence and added, "All I know is that I was a real butt toward you a little bit ago and I hope you can forgive me."

"In a heartbeat," Chrissi replied. "I never want to lose you."

"And if the job is still open, I would love to be your maid of honor," Rori offered.

Chrissi nodded. "It is, and I'm glad."

Tyler stared with a dumbfounded expression as Chrissi's words repeated in his mind. *We need to get counseling.* He found his voice as he pushed aside the tray of seedlings he'd been transplanting. "What are you talking about?"

They stood facing each other in the growing heat of the greenhouse; the late April sun pushing the interior temperature much warmer than the outdoor temperature. Chrissi had been surprised when she'd stepped inside and found Ty, clad in snug jeans and a clinging T-shirt that clearly showed well defined muscles. And now her mind skittered to the notion that she might be a very lucky girl after all.

The distraction had rattled Chrissi and she'd blurted, without preamble, "We need to get counseling." Of course, that would warrant the guarded look the man was now directing her way.

"Chris?"

Tyler waited, watching as his fiancée flushed with embarrassment. She glanced away and didn't seem to know what to say. He realized that he'd taken an intimidating stance, with his feet splayed and his arms crossed over his chest. He probably didn't look too open to conversation either, since she'd stepped unannounced into his greenhouse and looked him over like he was a contestant on one of those find-your-true-love-and-get-rich-at-the-same-time television game shows. His blood had heated as her appreciative gaze slid over his well-muscled frame and his body had jumped to natural conclusions about what should happen between them. He'd had to force his mind away – far away – from those thoughts, because their relationship was weeks or longer from that natural progression.

The silence throbbed, even after Tyler relaxed his stance. This was going nowhere. "Want to help me transplant some seedlings?" he asked as casually he could manage. "Take your jacket off and sit here," he indicated the stool that he'd vacated. "I'll set you up with a flat of cells to fill." She complied quietly. Tyler placed a fresh flat for himself on the table beside Chrissi's.

He pulled up a second stool and settled next to her. They performed the process of transplanting in silence, each knowing the job well. After a few minutes, she spoke. "I asked Rori Wheeler to be my maid of honor. You know – for the wedding."

"Uh-huh," Tyler responded. They continued to pull the seedlings from the starting tray and press them singly into the waiting cells of the four-packs. The fragile plants would grow and develop for a few more weeks before they would be ready to sell. When Chrissi didn't continue, he asked, "So the wedding is the reason we need counseling?"

She flashed a typical teenage girl look at him conveying a message that roughly meant, "You are *so* not funny." It also reminded him, that although Chrissi was an adult, she hadn't completely grown up yet.

"She's my closest friend." She wasn't looking at him now. "She wants what's best for me."

"I do, too," Tyler offered cautiously. "I love you."

A noise of derision escaped from Chrissi before she answered. "I told her that."

Ah-ha. "She doesn't approve?" he ventured.

His question was met with a shrug. She stood and lifted a filled flat. "Where do you want this?" she asked.

Tyler pointed to an open table where other freshly transplanted seedlings basked in the sun. "Grab another flat of empty cells on your way back," he suggested.

When she started on the second flat, he tried again to get Chrissi to tell him what was going on in her mind - besides the need for counseling. "So, is she willing to be in the wedding?"

"Maid of honor," she confirmed with a nod. Then locking onto his gaze, she explained, with a desperate quality in her voice, "She's my best friend. She knows me, Ty. Better than anyone else."

Frustrated, Tyler pushed aside the flats he'd been working on. "I can't read your mind, Chris. Just tell me what you came to say." He stepped away from the stool and paced to swap out the filled flat for an empty one.

She didn't speak until he stood close to her, with his hands tracing light paths along her shoulders. Even then, the girl kept her focus glued on the plants in front of her. "She figured out that I'm pregnant," she whispered.

Tyler rolled his shoulders and let his head drop back, gazing toward the sky as if looking for guidance. He'd agreed – he'd offered – to be the responsible one. He sighed, "So she told you what a jerk I am ..."

A smile curled the corners of her mouth when she finally turned and looked up. "Actually, she threatened to kill you," she surprised him with her honesty. "But I wouldn't let her."

"That's a relief," he countered. A smile touched his lips as he added, "I'm glad she was willing to champion your honor."

She looked at him then with tears filling her beautiful, sad brown eyes. "And she's glad you are willing to help me," she said cryptically. "But she thinks we can't handle this alone. Rori is certain that I need to see a counselor. And you need one, too."

Tyler gaped in response. "I think I'm old enough to be husband and a father without seeing a counselor," he replied with rising defensiveness. "She's 15! What could she know about it?"

"She's 16. And she could know a lot," Chrissi countered. "She watched her mother and Andrew self-destruct in their relationship."

"A lot of marriages fail."

"I don't want to fail; I want our relationship to have a chance," she pressed. "I want our marriage to last."

Tyler didn't see the relevance and shook off the idea. "Just because her parents couldn't hold it together doesn't mean we do can't do it."

Chrissi's next words brought back a long-forgotten piece of information. "Did you know Andrew isn't Rori's father?"

Tyler waited a beat, his lips tightening, before he nodded. "He was friends with Lucy in high school. People thought Rori might be his, but they both denied it," he related. "I think he was a sophomore when she was born ... that would have put me in sixth grade. I really wasn't paying any attention at that point."

"Rori said they got married when she was six," Chrissi contributed.

He nodded again. "Andrew went through hell trying to live with that woman," he said with a harshness that surprised Chrissi.

"Do you know why?"

"I don't want to talk about my friends," he said as he winced away from the topic. "If Rori tells you, that's her business because it's her family."

"She's afraid that I won't be able to return your love. She's worried that you won't be able to accept what happened to me," she whispered. "That's why she said I need counseling. She gave me the name and number for the doctor she has been seeing since her mother kidnapped her and Hope, and was killed trying to escape."

He turned, searching for a distraction. Too much, too emotional discussion was always stressful for him and he'd nearly reached the limit by simply thinking about spilling his thoughts and fears to a counselor. His voice was tight as the words scraped past his tongue, "We aren't going to fail, Chris. That's not going to happen."

"She might be right," Chrissi continued, as if she hadn't heard his protest. "But dealing with the circumstances – I don't know that we are prepared for that …"

"What are you talking about?" he demanded.

"I was raped," she rasped the words. "And we can't even say the word to each other. How will we build a life together?"

In the next milliseconds, Tyler wanted to run and scream, kick and hit things, but the fear and vulnerability exuding from

Chrissi stopped him from reacting. More reassurance. More love. More kindness. More understanding. More, more, more. Did he have enough "more" to give her? Would she be able to give back at some point? God, he hoped so.

"Chris, honey," he whispered, as he pulled her to her feet and held her close. He cradled her head against his shoulder. He breathed in her scent, closed his eyes and rocked her gently. "I can talk about it if you're ready. But I'm never going to push you for details."

"How can you be so understanding all the time? And strong?" she pondered as she pulled back to look into his eyes.

"I'm not," he denied. "I get scared and worried, too. I don't know what's going to happen." He pulled her close again and buried his face in her hair and whispered, "I love you. And I trust God. But I wish that baby really was mine, and I wish you didn't have to live with the thoughts of what happened to you. I wish I didn't have fears of my own. I wish we could have had a traditional start, but that's simply not the way things are."

"If wishes were horses, then beggars would ride," she responded thinking of the phrase a former English teacher used to quote. And then she recalled Rori's advice, that Tyler would be needing love and support from her – that she would need to contribute to the relationship, not simply take what Tyler was willing to give. "I can help you with some of your concerns, Ty," she sniffled.

"How?"

Chrissi locked onto his gaze. "Some of your fears come from the unknown. And it was selfish of me not to give you the information you need."

"You're not selfish," he argued. "Not in the slightest."

Amazingly, the story flowed from Chrissi's lips as she and Tyler sat side by side on a greenhouse bench. His arm wrapped protectively around her shoulders, and at times tears slipped silently down his cheeks. She explained that she'd been given some sort of drug that had rendered her unconscious, so she did not have any memory of being assaulted.

Periodically he'd let an oath escape and pull her closer. Tyler had railed about his failure to follow her and return her to Miller's Bend before she got so far as Chicago. "Matt thought I'd gone off the deep end, because I was pushing him to go after you," he confided. "I was worried the whole time you were gone and now I know it was right to be worried. I prayed for God to protect you …"

She laid a soft hand against Tyler's darkly whiskered cheek and stroked lightly. "And He did protect me."

"How?" he demanded harshly. "How can you say he protected you?"

"Agent Stockard." Her brows drew down in confusion, "Didn't you hear how many ways he helped me?"

"You should never have gone through that," he growled.

"I could have been drugged and raped repeatedly, instead of only once," she countered. "Stockard protected me when he could, and he gave me knowledge to help myself when he couldn't be there. The man risked his life to bring me a Bible because he understood that the Word would help me cope." Her expression was almost accusatory as her gaze locked on Tyler's. "He also died trying to protect me, here in the police station."

"My own father almost died doing the same." Tyler's voice had been cold and hard as steel when the words slid out. Scenes from the day of the shooting bombarded Tyler and his grip tightened on Chrissi as he remembered her terrified reactions.

"You wouldn't let us comfort you …" he recalled. "Matt and I tried, but you kept backing away and Ashley – she made us go help the others." His gaze caught on Chrissi's anxious expression. "Did she know? *Does* she know?"

Chrissi shook her head. "Nobody knew, except for me and Agent Stockard." She paused. "And Slug."

Dazed and confused, Tyler was trying to assimilate the information. "Who?"

"The shooter," she informed him in a detached way. "He was the man who raped me, according to Stockard."

CHAPTER EIGHTEEN

Jeff Schuster had been worrying about his son. In recent days, an awkwardness had begun to open up between Tyler and Chrissi. He glanced at the clock in his office … 10 p.m. on a Saturday night wasn't usually a busy time in the Miller's Bend police department. But this was prom night, and he had scheduled three patrolmen, including himself, to increase visibility and hopefully deter some of the party-goers from drinking and driving. He was busy catching up on the endless stream of paperwork until he would be needed on the streets.

He'd considered asking Tyler what was going on with Chrissi, but the man was a grown up and didn't need his father meddling in his business. "Lord, I hope they didn't mess this up," he whispered as he flipped a folder closed and reached for the next one.

In response to a knock from the doorway, the chief raised his focus and a smile spread across his features when he recognized Tyler. "Hey," he said in welcome.

"Hey, Dad." Tyler continued to lean against the door frame. He glanced at the clock and fidgeted. "You got a minute?"

Jeff closed the folder he had just opened and placed it back in the pile he'd taken it from. "About 30 of 'em before the kids start slipping away from the dance and the cruising begins.

Come on in." He gestured toward the chair by the wall, rather than the ones that stood starkly in front of his desk.

Clad in his EMT uniform, Tyler moved slowly toward the chair. "You're on duty?" his father asked as Tyler lowered himself into the soft cushions. The ambulance garage was part of the city office complex and it was common practice for the EMTs to pass time with the police officers if they weren't out on calls. Tyler closed his eyes and nodded as he let the fatigue pull his head back against the wall. "Until midnight," he confirmed. "I hate prom night," he added.

"I don't recall that you actually ever went to the prom," his father observed passively.

Tyler rocked his head back and forth. "Never wanted to go," he admitted. "But this year … Chrissi's there and I couldn't go so I volunteered to take the shift."

The younger man felt the intensity of the chief's gaze. "You think that was wise? I mean considering that you're going on, what is it? About 22 hours of duty without a break?"

Tyler nodded and pulled his eyes open to face his father. "I've pulled double shifts before. Besides, I didn't want to go stalking the teenagers at the prom." He stood and began to skulk around the large antique wooden desk that had been Chief Schuster's command post for decades.

"So she went without you?"

"I couldn't go, Dad," Tyler's frustration echoed in his voice. "You have to be a high school senior or junior, or dating one if you're younger, to participate in the prom. You know that." He narrowed a glare at his father, "In fact I think that rule was recommended by the police chief a few years back."

Jeff ignored the jibe. "Who's her … escort?" Jeff asked, wondering if there was a serious problem in the relationship. In an attempt to lighten the mood, he added, "I could have the joker arrested."

Tyler's sigh wasn't light at all. "Nice try. Her date is Josh Pendleton's kid brother, Jake. They are kind of doubling with Rori and Daniel Fields. Actually, the only way Andrew would let Rori go was if Chrissi agreed to be sure she got delivered safely to his parents' farm, since he and Allison are out of town on business." He faced his father and added with gloomy seriousness, "And, no, I don't want Jake arrested."

"I could intimidate him a little ..."

The longing in his son's gaze cracked Jeff's heart a little bit. "Everything alright between you two?"

Tyler shrugged and picked up a knife-like letter opener from the desk. He tossed and caught it, flipping it as if he were a knife-thrower in a sideshow. "I just wish ..." his voice trailed away. There was no way his dad would understand.

The warmth of his father's hand on his shoulder stilled the butterflies in Tyler's stomach. His words helped calm Tyler's jangled nerves. "Prom is a big night for the girls, and you wish you could be the one to share it with her," Jeff said with unexpected understanding. "She's alright, you know."

Tyler nodded. He began pacing again, and flipping the letter opener.

"Something else on your mind?" Jeff guessed.

"She thinks we need counseling," Tyler blurted without a chance to censor the thought. Distress was evident in his features as he made the revelation. "I mean, we haven't even gotten married yet, and she's so sure that we'll mess it up that we need to see a doctor. What's that say about me? About us?"

Jeff regarded his son and let the question swirl in his mind before answering. "It means she's a smart girl," he began to answer, but stopped when Tyler spun toward him.

"So you have no faith in me either?" he demanded without conviction.

"I have infinite faith in you. And in her, too," Jeff contradicted. "You need to trust her judgment -"

"I'm trying!" Jeff yelled as he drove the sharp tip of the letter opener into the desk. And then more quietly, he added in a strangled voice, "I'm trying, Dad."

Jeff watched the end of the letter opener quiver from the vibration of piercing the surface of the desk, and then cleared his throat. "You know, that *is* mahogany," he stated flatly.

Tyler burst out in laughter. "Like one more gouge matters," he said seconds later.

"Right," Jeff confirmed. "It's a little thing that doesn't matter. That ding doesn't change my desk by even one small fraction."

Tyler just stared at his father, confused, but certain there was a message in there somewhere. "It's been a really long day ... could you just spell out what you want me to understand, please?"

"Nothin'. It's just that the dents and scrapes on the desk don't change the function of the desk," Jeff explained without explaining.

"Fine. It's a desk."

"Going to counseling doesn't change your feelings, son," Jeff said as he reached for the light switch. With a nod toward the door, he expounded, "If your woman thinks that she needs to talk something out, then she needs to talk it out. It isn't going to change her feelings for you. And it sure as shooting isn't going to change your feelings for her."

He ushered Tyler through the doorway and pulled the door closed behind him. As Tyler moved ahead of Jeff through the hallway that would lead him back to the ambulance bay, he thought he heard his father add with a chuckle, "Unless you're knuckle-headed enough to make a mountain out of a mole hill."

Chrissi pulled her cell phone from the clutch purse that lay on the table at the sidelines of the dance floor. She shouldn't have come to the prom, she'd decided about 20 minutes after the grand march. She was tired and she missed Tyler and she didn't want to be here anymore.

A few days had passed since she and Tyler sat in the sunny warmth of the greenhouse and she'd disclosed the story of her time in Chicago. To her surprise he had appeared to handle that pretty well. But when she'd talked about the need to see a counselor, he hadn't really warmed to the idea. Ha! He'd dug in his heels like a yearling calf being halter broke in preparation for the show ring. No way did he want to go to counseling.

Tonight Chrissi had decided that she could live without counseling, but she didn't want to live without Tyler. So she would call him when his shift ended at midnight and tell him that it was alright, she'd given up the idea of seeing Dr. Kingston. Maybe that would help dispel some of the tension between them.

She checked the time, relieved to see that they should be leaving in about 10 minutes in order to get Rori to her grandparents' farm in the country by the curfew Andrew had set for his daughter. She typed out a quick text to Tyler, *Wish you were here ... or I was there. I love you.* She closed her phone and slipped it inside her bag. He wouldn't read the message until he was off duty, but at least it would be there as soon as he could get to it. And it made her feel closer to him.

Happiness and excitement danced in Rori's eyes as she returned to their table with Daniel in tow. "This is great!" she shouted above the music of the live band. "Can we stay longer?"

Chrissi shook her head and pointed to the spot on her wrist where a watch would have been. "We need to get you to your grandparents." She looked around trying to locate her date, but didn't see him among the throng of swaying bodies. "Where's Jake?"

Rori looked sheepish and Daniel glanced away with a shrug.

"Come on guys," Chrissi spoke sharply. "I don't care who he's dancing with, we just need to leave."

"I'll see if he'll give up the car keys," Daniel suggested. "I can drive you ladies home and come back for him." Chrissi nodded and the boy disappeared into the crowd. Rori alighted in the chair next to Chrissi in a swirl of satin and tulle and lace.

Her expression shown with excitement as Rori seemed to bask in the fantasy of the event. "I'm so glad I could come here tonight," Rori confided to Chrissi, as if it were a closely-held secret. "Isn't Daniel hot?"

Chrissi nodded. "I hope your hottie comes back quickly. We need to get going," she said as she surveyed the mass of bodies wrapped in shimmering dresses and dashing tuxes. Just then Mr. Hottie slipped past Chrissi, coming from behind her to stand next to Rori.

"Jake won't give me the keys," he reported with annoyance. "And he won't leave because … well, he won't leave."

Chrissi pushed her chair back and stood. "I don't care. We are leaving. Rori and I can walk to my place and I'll take her back out to her grandparents' place," she said. Meeting Daniel's eyes she explained, "Your car is at your grandmother's, right? You can just walk there and then ... do whatever." She picked up her clutch and began moving through the crowd toward the exit.

As they left through the main doors of the school, the old superintendent, Mr. Jones, reminded the trio roughly that if they left the dance, they would not be allowed to return. Rori cast a longing glance behind her toward the sounds and lights of the temporary wonderland that had been created in the gym. But it was Daniel who answered with a sense of inflated chivalry, "We understand. But I've promised to see the ladies safely home before their curfews."

Mr. Jones raised an eyebrow as his glance veered to Chrissi and rebounded quickly to the young man. "Of course you have. Hope you all had a good time tonight."

As they began walking west, a path that would separate Daniel from the girls, he suggested, "We can all walk to my Grandma's and I will take you home. You don't need to walk all the way to Mrs. Holmes' place."

Rori teetered slightly on her high heeled shoes and Daniel quickly steadied her. Chrissi nodded. The idea made sense, and her feet were already starting to hurt. And nobody had wrapped an arm around her for the walk home. She pulled her cell phone from the bag again to check for messages from Ty, but she knew there would be none. He was still on duty. The time alarmed her, though. "Rori," she said as she extended her hand that held the phone toward the younger girl. "You'd better call your

207

grandparents … we aren't going to make it out there on time and I don't want them to worry."

Tyler's pulse raced when the radio crackled to life. He glanced at the clock as he and his partner headed for the rig. Less than an hour remained on his shift and he'd have been off for the night. He could have stopped by her apartment to see Chrissi, gone home and crashed. But an ambulance call on prom night had the potential to become a horrific nightmare. He jumped into the passenger seat as the senior EMT, Duane, claimed the driver's position. *Please, God, don't let it be a fatality.*

The overhead garage door hadn't reached its apex by the time Duane had the rig rolling toward the expanding opening. Tyler's hands froze in the act of securing his seat belt when he heard the destination broadcast over the radio: the intersection of Highway 212 and 452nd Avenue. Less than two miles from the home of Riley's parents. In a small town, it is common for the emergency responders to come upon accidents and emergencies where they are well acquainted with the victims, and Tyler hoped this would not be one of those times.

The sirens wailed as Duane guided the emergency vehicle through the town and out onto the open highway, headed west, toward the accident scene. Additional information was relayed from the dispatcher: reported by a civilian who remained on the scene; one-car roll-over; two victims, one ambulatory male, one unconscious female; a deputy was on the scene; Sheriff Dunn and the fire department's rescue squad were en route, as well as the ambulance and a wrecker.

They saw the eerie flash of the rescue vehicles' lights before they reached the intersection. Seconds before they'd turned off the highway, Dunn's voice sounded over the radio asking dispatch to contact the police chief and have him call Dunn on his cell phone. The request struck Tyler as odd, but before he could dwell on it, Dunn added a curt "10-3" order to dispatch and the radio fell silent. Tyler looked to his more experienced partner and asked, "Stop transmitting? What's that for?"

"No idea," the older man answered as he made the turn onto the gravel road and maneuvered the ambulance around the other emergency vehicle to get positioned as close to the subject vehicle as they could get. It was an older Buick which lay on its roof in the ditch, Tyler focused on the job at hand: assess the victims, stabilize and transport to the hospital.

In unison, he and Duane circled to the back doors of the vehicle to position the power gurney behind the vehicle. Tyler grabbed the backboard and C-collar, while Duane grasped the emergency kit and began leading the way toward Dunn who was the incident commander. Tyler's mind took in more of the scene as they approached the hub of activity. Harsh flood lights had been set up to illuminate the area, corrupting the colors and dramatizing the movements by the rescue workers. The ambulatory male victim was standing by an older man who Tyler recognized in an instant as Riley's father.

Dunn held a cell phone to his ear, but as he registered the arrival of the ambulance crew, he disconnected the call and strode deliberately to intercept the pair. The young sheriff's expression was tight as if this was a particularly bad situation. Tyler's mind grasped the building oddities, including the request for radio silence, and although it was really Duane's position to ask questions, he opened his mouth to ask what on Earth was going on.

Before the words broke free, the screech of metal being ripped apart cut through the night air, followed by shouts from the rescue squad. Dunn's serious expression darkened further as he extended a hand toward Tyler's chest. "Hold up," he ordered roughly. Turning to Duane, he added, "The deputy will assist you with … the primary victim. Tyler's going to take the boy."

The backboard and C-collar were stripped from Tyler's grip by a uniformed man Tyler didn't even bother to look at. The strangled emotions in his friend's expression had caused Tyler's chest to constrict. He hadn't known Erik to ever feel or show emotion at an accident scene before. Something was wrong. "What is it?" Tyler scratched the question past his tightening throat. "*Who* is it?" he demanded.

Seconds ticked by as Erik swallowed hard, but he didn't look away from Tyler's gaze. "It's Chrissi."

It's Chrissi. The words echoed in his mind and ricocheted to his heart where his pain magnified. And the baby. He had to go to her; he had to help them. Tyler's powerful body shot past the sheriff, following the path Duane and the deputy had taken. Erik's hand pulled him back, spinning Tyler to face him, "You can't go over there," he commanded. "You need to see to the ambulatory victim."

"She's pregnant," Tyler blurted in a broken statement, "Tell them. You have to tell them!" Erik responded with an oath, and after repeating the command to Tyler take over the care of Daniel, he sprinted to the other side of the car where rescuers worked to free Chrissi from the car and stabilize her.

Tears blurred Tyler's vision and he knew in the flash of that second that nothing in the world mattered more to him than the woman who lay unconscious in the early May night and their child. Mere yards lay between the spot where they struggled for life and the isolated place where he stood, but his family was completely out of his reach. He was helpless to assist in any way. "Please God … Please."

When he would have taken a step to follow, a heavy hand upon Tyler's shoulder stopped him. He closed his eyes against the anguish and steeled himself. He was a professional and his skills were needed. Pushing away imagined images of Chrissi, he turned his focus to the other victim, and turned to face the man who had stopped him from following Erik. Riley's father, Lawrence Wheeler, stood with an arm wrapped around the teenage boy's shoulders as if to keep Daniel from bolting, and each wore an expression as if his world was spinning out of control.

Tyler inhaled deeply, trying to focus on his victim. "Let's get you checked out," he said as he led Daniel to the rear of the ambulance. He seated the young man on the waiting gurney and fitted him with a C-collar before beginning a field evaluation. Tyler winced as sounds carried to his ears on the night air – a stray word or exclamation, more sounds of metal being pulled apart, a cry of pain that chilled his blood. Each time he jumped, Lawrence would steady his nerves with a hand to the shoulder or a word of support.

Finally, Tyler could tell that they'd gotten Chrissi onto the backboard and would be moving her to the ambulance. He told Daniel that he would need to be evaluated at the hospital, but didn't seem to have any life-threatening injuries. Tyler moved his victim to the passenger seat of the ambulance and closed the door.

He turned to find Lawrence continuing to shadow him. "Thanks," Tyler whispered.

"No problem," he rasped out in response. "Any word on Rori?" he asked with tears standing in his own eyes. Rori was his first grandchild and everyone knew that Lawrence and Rori had a special bond.

Confusion controlled Tyler's response for a second. He remembered Dunn's request to dispatch to have the police chief call his cell; he remembered the radio silence order; he remembered the torment in Dunn's eyes when they'd arrived on scene. And a new fear swept through him, he asked cautiously, "What about Rori?"

"She's gone ..." the older man answered, but then his shoulders jumped in a half-controlled sob. "That low-life took her." Tyler clasped his friend's father in a brief embrace of shared fears and anger.

Tyler's voice was sharp when the question slipped past his lips. "Who?"

Lawrence stepped back and glanced toward their farm, just over a mile down the road. "Daniel and Chrissi were bringing Rori to us after the dance, 'cause her folks are out of town," he began to explain. "Daniel says a big pickup followed them when he turned off the highway." The older man's focus traveled back to Tyler's face as he spoke. "Says the guy forced them off the gravel road and then, instead of helping them, he took Rori."

A roar of anger, frustration, and injustice tore from Tyler's throat as he spun, slamming his hands against the side of the ambulance. A tragic accident would have been hard enough to bear, but this? This had been done intentionally! The thought was horrific. What kind of person wreaks that kind of pain and damage on other people? And why? When he focused again on Lawrence's face, Tyler demanded, "Who did this?!"

With a nod toward Daniel, ensconced in the cab of the ambulance, he revealed, "He says it was Adam Brewer."

CHAPTER NINETEEN

Tyler had never been known for his patience. And this night in particular had seemed to drag on for days. Of course, if he hadn't been coming off of a 24-hour shift, it might have been a little better. The night had been filled with frustrations and fears. And anger. And loneliness. And prayer.

With his head cradled against the palms of his hands, elbows braced on his knees, Tyler let his eyes droop closed as images of the night just past replayed in his mind. He'd seen her, held her hand and kissed her forehead, assuring his unconscious fiancée that he loved her, that she'd be fine and that their baby would be fine. But as Erik pulled Tyler back and the others loaded the gurney into the ambulance, he'd seen with horror that blood stained the light blanket covering her. Blood where there shouldn't have been any.

He shivered at the memory, as the pain ignited by the very thought that they could lose their baby crashed over him again. At the scene of the accident, Tyler had moved to climb into the ambulance with Chrissi, but Erik stopped him. "Duane will ride with her; the deputy will drive," he'd explained with quiet authority. "You're coming with me."

Helplessly, Tyler had watched as the ambulance left the scene, lights flashing against the black of night, sirens echoing in the void. Anguish echoing in his soul.

Erik had taken him to the ambulance garage, where he told Tyler to change out of his uniform and try to relax before heading to the hospital. The man went so far as to advise Tyler to go home and get some rest, although there was no conviction in the suggestion.

Once he'd arrived at the hospital, Tyler had been denied any information about Chrissi until Melanie and Byron arrived. Melanie had given the hospital staff permission to include Tyler in all updates about Chrissi's condition. Tyler's father had stopped in briefly to lend support, but he hadn't been able to stay long because of Rori's disappearance. As the police chief, he was the lead officer in the investigation. The girl's safe return would clearly be the priority in Jeff's life. Until she was returned safely to her family, Tyler was on his own. The people Tyler had always counted on to help him center his thoughts were all unavailable. His father was working, Mrs. Holmes was home asleep, as she should be, Chrissi was hospitalized, and Matt … Where was Matt anyway? He should have been there with the rest of them, waiting for word about Chrissi.

Tyler raised his head, zeroing his focus on his soon-to-be-mother-in-law. Only one month into remission after cancer treatments, she was showing the strain of spending the night in the hospital waiting room, worrying about her child … her children. "Melanie?" he rasped out, drawing her attention from across the waiting room. If it was possible, she looked even more frightened than Tyler felt. She met his gaze but didn't speak. "Where's Matt?"

She took on a hollow look, as if she couldn't face the question, and then she turned away. Dropping her focus first to her hands and, finding no answer there, she slowly looked into the face of her former husband. She began to cry. Again.

It was Byron who answered the question, "We're not sure. He and Ashley haven't answered their cell phones or their land line. I even drove over there - no one was home. Not at the studio either." He shook his head despondently. "And they haven't returned any calls."

The redundancy irritated Tyler. He knew they weren't answering the phones, because he'd been trying to call Matt as well. *Where are you, Matt? Chrissi needs you – we all need you.*

Silence returned, letting Tyler's thoughts wander. He needed something to focus on or he was going to lose his mind. Early in the vigil, he'd slipped from the waiting room to his pickup and returned with the manuscript Ashley had given him. And so he had picked up the loose sheets of paper and he'd begun to read the story that his grandmother was so certain he needed to know.

Tyler became engrossed in the reading and lost track of time until Dr. Stapp stepped into the room. The trio clamored to their feet, eager for an update, but the doctor's message was brief and he was there just long enough to tell them that Chrissi was stable. He'd somberly concluded that no one would see Chrissi until morning. And, once again, Tyler, was told to go home. Melanie and Byron didn't heed the advice any better than Tyler did, he thought as the threesome settled in to wait. Not patiently.

During the pre-dawn hours a body slipped into the chair adjacent to Tyler's. He'd been absorbed in Mrs. Holmes' book and was surprised to see Pastor Mark when he looked up. "What are you doing here?" Tyler asked roughly.

"Couldn't sleep," the kind-eyed man answered. Pastor Mark, at around Andrew's age, somehow exuded a calm wisdom that was completely unreasonable for someone so young.

"So you thought you'd check out the hospital waiting rooms?" Tyler challenged skeptically. And then as if it was an accusation, he added, "Somebody called you."

"You called me," the pastor said softly.

Tyler's breath caught for a second, and then he laughed and shook his head. "Matt's the only one I called."

"Not hardly." After a pause, Mark asked Tyler to bring him up to speed on the situation. And after he had done so, Mark spoke quietly. "No wonder I couldn't sleep."

"I don't know how long I can sit here and do nothing," Tyler hissed in a whispered tone. Agony crossed his features before he confessed, "I need to see Chris; I want to help find Rori, and right now I'd happily kill the Brewer kid if I laid eyes on him." He looked away as the honesty in his statement registered. The windows of the waiting room were still darkened by the night sky and they would be for another hour, at least, before the first flares of dawn's light would begin to push the darkness back and away.

Pastor Mark's soothing voice reached a raw place in Tyler's mind. "Better a patient man than a warrior," he quoted with a Biblical tone. "It's better to be a man who controls his temper than one who takes a city."

Tyler knew the man meant well, but there are times when hearing quotes from the Bible, taken out of context, can be downright annoying. And this was one of them. "I don't want to 'take a city'," he countered. "I want Chris to be alright. I want her to be safe and healthy." He stopped speaking when his throat constricted. Tears threatened to spill over onto his cheeks.

He paced to the window, and let his forehead rest against it. The coolness of the hard surface seemed to take the edge off the dull headache that he hadn't even realized he had. He waited, soaking in the dulcifying effect. The pastor's hand settled on his shoulder, but Tyler didn't acknowledge the man's presence.

"What else?" Mark finally asked quietly. When Tyler refused to answer, he repeated the question saying, "What else? There has to be more."

The couple had been taking the accelerated marriage class with Pastor Mark so they would be ready to wed in early June. The pastor was aware of the pregnancy, but not the details. Like almost everyone else, he assumed that the child was Tyler's.

Tyler glanced across the room to see that Chrissi's parents seemed to be asleep and wouldn't hear his next words. "Our baby," Tyler answered on a ragged breath. "Chris was bleeding when they put her in the ambulance," he confided. "I don't know ..."

"Good Lord."

"What if we lose the baby?" He asked brokenly. "What if she's already gone, and I don't even know it?"

"You can't -" Mark began but his voice broke. He swallowed hard and continued, "You can't think that way. You have to stay positive. Be of good courage and the Lord will strengthen your heart."

"My heart is fine -"

"Your heart is breaking," the pastor argued gently. "You need to refill it with love and prayer, not what-ifs and doubts."

"I've got medical training. I'm not naïve," Tyler declared as bitterness surged in his voice. "There's a very real possibility …"

"And if that happens, you and Chrissi will survive," Mark declared with the assurance of a man backed by God. "Your love and dedication to the Lord, and to each other, can see you through events like that. But unless it happens, don't spend your energies there."

Insecurities rippled through Tyler. "Maybe it's punishment …"

"What?" the pastor seemed incredulous. "You're implying that God would snuff out an innocent life which he has created? Just to teach someone a lesson?"

Tyler shrugged.

"Don't be so hard-headed, Tyler," Mark admonished. "Our God is a creator. He loves life and tells us that children are a heritage from Him." He turned Tyler to face him full-on. "If you lose the baby, do not take counsel from anyone who tries to tell you it was God's will. I don't believe He works that way and neither do you."

"Doesn't He?"

"No," Mark repeated. "If you lose the baby, it is a result of an act of man – not an act of God." Placing a stabilizing hand to Tyler's shoulder, he added, "The actions of man will never take you to a place where the grace of God cannot reach you."

Tyler didn't respond, but found comfort in Pastor Mark's words. Melanie and Byron stirred, and the pastor spoke with them, but left soon afterward, saying that he needed some time for himself before the Sunday morning services. Tyler decided the man was right, at least about focusing on something positive. Like trying to help find Rori. If only Matt were there with him, they could talk through the problem and come up with some ideas.

Matt, with his need to control everything, should be all over the staff demanding answers. He should be crazy to find and punish the man who had caused the accident – the man who had injured Matt's baby sister and made his mother cry. Why hadn't he showed up at the hospital? Why hadn't he called? And what about Ashley? She hadn't returned any of the messages that Melanie had left for her either. Even if she wasn't interested as a family member, the reporter's instinct in her should be consumed with covering this incident.

If Tyler had been the kind of person who would wish an eternity of purgatory on a person, he decided that Adam Brewer would be among the damned. Tyler smirked as he thought of the derelict adrift in a sea of lost souls for perpetuity – yeah, that's the ticket – a lifetime of nothing. That would teach Brewer a lesson. Maybe, Tyler thought with amusement, he would add an extra fifty-thousand years for attacking Rori and scaring her – the first time; and a couple hundred-thousand more years for stealing her away last night. The thought of doling out punishment to the little pinheaded delinquent was growing in appeal and Tyler went for the figurative cherry on top by adding another million years for pain and suffering. That would serve him right. He'd never go after anybody again. Maybe, Tyler thought, he would add an additional thousand years for breaking into the Chronicle and vandalizing the place.

It's amazing what sleep deprivation will do for a person's mind. And it was in that moment, several components linked together clearly: Adam and Rori; Adam and the Chronicle;

Ashley and the Chronicle; Ashley and Matt; Matt's not at the hospital because … he can't be.

Seconds later he was listening to the voicemail message on his father's phone. In frustration, Tyler hit the end button and dialed the sheriff's office. When the dispatcher answered, Tyler's words were sharper than he'd have liked. "Patch me through to the chief," he ordered.

"What's your business," came the smoke-roughened voice that he recognized as Sylvie. The woman had been the head dispatcher since Tyler was knee-high to a grasshopper and she had always seemed to think she could mother him along a bit.

He bit back a curse and ran a hand through his hair in agitation. "Just put me through," he demanded.

"Tyler? Is that you boy?" she asked, turning the tables on him. "I thought we straightened this out years ago. You can't call through the emergency -"

The oath escaped from his lips, interrupting her narrative. "Sylvie! Patch me through now! It could be life or death!"

A startled silence followed. Suddenly his father's voice boomed in Tyler's ear, "What?"

"I'm not positive, but I think Brewer has Rori at the office of the Chronicle," he blurted in reply. "We haven't been able to get a hold of Ashley or Matt all night. Brewer may have them, too."

Improbable though it was, Tyler must have succumbed to the exhaustion that had pulled at his mind, because the next thing he knew for certain was that someone was touching his shoulder.

"Bro?" a familiar voice beckoned him toward consciousness. Tyler forced himself to respond with a slight nod. And then dragging his heavy eyelids open, he registered the expression of remorse in Matt's face. "Sorry I wasn't here with you all last night," he offered in a low voice. An ironic half-smile altered his expression as he added, "But I was a little tied up." He extended his right hand toward Tyler as if to clasp his hand and pull him to his feet.

Tyler automatically reached for the hand, but froze when he saw bandage wrapped around Matt's wrist. He surged to his feet, grabbing for Matt's left hand where he found more of the same. Feeling a bit disoriented, Tyler's gaze shot to his friend's face. "What the …?"

"Bobbie and Adam Brewster," Matt replied morosely. As if that fully explained everything that had happened. "You saved our lives when you called your dad and sent him to the newspaper office." He picked up the package which held the pages that comprised Mrs. Holmes' book and handed it to Tyler.

Tyler's mind was quickly bringing back the long night and his heart skipped to the woman he loved. "Chris! Have you seen her?" His focus swept the room and discovered that Melanie and Byron had disappeared. "Where are your folks?"

Tyler finally noticed the grotesque swelling and angry bruising on Matt's face and started to ask about it, but his friend cut him off. "That can wait. Ashley, Rori and I are all okay – thanks to you." He paused, looking away before he continued, "I've been in to see Chrissi, but she's asking for you." Matt pulled in a slow breath and rubbed his large hand gingerly across his ribs, and winced in response to the pressure. "Mom and Byron are headed for home. I told Chrissi I'd deliver you to her before I take Ashley home."

"Where is she?" he asked, but Matt was already leading the way. Silently they passed out of the waiting room. They paced down the long quiet corridor and before turning the corner that would lead to the room in which Chrissi had been settled, Tyler stopped his friend. Many words jumbled in his mind and choked in his throat, but only two passed his lips in a barely audible whisper, "The baby?"

Tyler's expectant gaze was met with a sad smile from his friend. "Talk with Chrissi. Everything is going to be fine," Matt replied without answering the real question. "Second door on the left." He turned and was gone.

Everything is going to be fine. The words echoed in Tyler's mind as he stepped into the doorway. Fear that he would pass out flickered through his consciousness as he moved to the bedside. She lay on her side facing the entrance, he noted. Chrissi's eyes were closed, her face relaxed, her dark hair was pulled back in a ponytail or maybe a braid. Her head rested on the pillow, with her pale skin nearly blending with the color of the sterile cotton bedding. Her ribcage raised and lowered in steady breathing pattern, and monitoring equipment hummed and beeped.

He didn't want to disturb Chrissi, but the desire to touch her won over the limited self-control he possessed at that moment. He hated the way his hand shook as he reached, ever so slowly to run his fingertips along the velvety skin where the fine baby hairs edged her face. *Everything is going to be fine,* the voice repeated in his head. But in his heart, he questioned whether the aftermath of the accident would tear them apart.

Bending closer, Tyler pledged in a hoarse whisper, "I love you more than life. I'm so sorry …" His words stopped, but his heart cried out in agony. He swallowed hard more than once and a tear dropped onto the pillow. "I should have been with you. I should have been able to help you." His lips gently brushed the soft skin above her temple, as his fingers slipped in a loving path down past her jawline to the sensitive skin along Chrissi's neck. "I'll never let you down again. I love you more than you can understand – more than I can understand. Just don't let this be the end. I love you."

Chrissi's sleep-deprived, medication-laden mind was slowly waking from the sweet dream. The deep voice that she knew instinctively as Tyler's whispered about love, and sorrow. Her brow creased in confusion even though she hadn't come fully awake. She'd been dreaming of their baby – sweet and innocent, chubby and smiling – and now Tyler's low voice sounded deeply sad, regretful. His fingers skimmed her skin, awakening her senses and his lips touched her face. He'd promised to be happy about the baby, to love it. But he sounded remorseful. Why would he sound so sad?

Chrissi forced her mind to surge toward consciousness; she willed her muscles to follow her orders. Finally, her hand grasped his wrist and she forced her eyes open. Tyler's ministrations ceased as his gaze locked on Chrissi's eyes and the emotions she saw there reflected and magnified her own and the intensity of them crashed over her. Never, ever, had she dreamed that she would feel so much for another person – that she could feel so much of another person's soul.

Suspended away from reality, they clung to each other. Neither speaking. Neither moving. Conveying so much without words. Chrissi didn't know how much time had passed when they became aware of another person entering the room. As if they shared the same instinct, Tyler loosened his hold on her. She raised the head of the bed, so she was sitting and Tyler met the gaze of the doctor who stood just inside the now-closed door. Tyler's hand tightened around hers as if clinging to each other could ward off everything bad that could come to them.

She would later realize that Tyler hadn't been ashamed of his tears or the raw emotions in his eyes. He hadn't tried to cover them up or disguise them as anything other than the expressions of love and fear that they were.

"Sorry to interrupt," Dr. Stapp began in a polite tone. "There are some things we should go over." Before he finished his sentence he was paged to the emergency room. "Sorry. This will have to wait," he said as he left the room, pulling the door closed behind him.

Tyler nodded solemnly but didn't speak. Chrissi looked to him for assurance, and found none – only an escalating look of despair. It was a foreign air about him, and the effect was frightening to her. Rori's advice came back to her: *Tyler's going to need some of that love and support back sometimes.*

She also remembered a verse from the Bible that had confounded Chrissi when she'd read it days earlier: "Do not forsake her, and she will keep you; love her, and she will guard you." It hadn't made sense at the time, because she'd been thinking of the man as the caregiver. But it flashed in her mind that Tyler needed her, just as badly as she needed him.

He hadn't faltered in his caring for her; he'd stood up for Chrissi. He'd offered to stand with her, and he'd supported her even when she hadn't wanted him to. Tyler had not forsaken her, not for a second. And now it was her time to guard him – to shore up his emotional footings.

"Ty," she sighed and tugged at his hand to get his attention. When he looked back to Chrissi she was taken aback to read the torment in his expression. Contrary to her increasing fears, she strove for confidence in her voice when she spoke. "It's okay. I promise we are going to be alright."

She urged him to bend closer and he complied. Locking her gaze on Tyler's silver-gray eyes, Chrissi was reminded of a lost child. He was a person in need of reassurance and help finding his way back to home and safety. Lifting her hand she skimmed the rough stubble of his beloved face, finally cupping his cheek. She willed him to understand the depth of her love as she repeated, "I love you, Tyler. This accident was nothing – just a bump in the road. I'll be out of here in a few days and we'll move forward with our plans."

A sick unease rolled through Chrissi when he didn't respond. He sat next to her on the bed, facing her. Dropped a hand to her far hip and closed his eyes. When he opened them again, Tyler seemed to have driven some of his demons into retreat, but there was a hint of coldness in his expression. "That's what you want?" he rasped the words. "Just go on as if nothing happened?"

Bewildered, Chrissi frowned as she nodded slowly. "Nothing important did happen," she protested. "Nothing's changed." Tears were quickly building in Chrissi's eyes, along with the feeling of anxious torment which amplified within her heart. "I love you; you love me. We'll get married and have the life God has directed us toward."

"How …" Tyler choked on a response. As much as she tried to reassure him, it seemed that every word Chrissi said served to deepen his torment. *Please, God, help him listen to my heart.* Suddenly, on instinct, she grasped Tyler's hand that rested at her hip and slipped it to the left. It glided over the bony protrusion that was her hip bone, a few more inches and his strong, calloused palm rested atop her lower abdomen, where the child they loved rested.

The baby had grown in the weeks since he'd first touched it so adoringly, and he hadn't brought it up since. She hadn't thought to repeat that particular act again, but now she remembered the sweet reverence he'd responded with when he'd felt the small firm knot that would be their child.

Today his reaction was different though. Tyler resisted, as soon as he realized where his hand rested. When he would have pulled away, Chrissi secured his hand beneath both of hers. The tears that had hung in her eyes overflowed. "We need you," she pleaded.

Tyler's fears resurfaced with a vengeance and he looked away. When he turned his head back toward her, his focus wasn't on her eyes as he spoke. "The accident," he began, but faltered and had to swallow hard before starting in again. "You were bleeding -"

"I'm fine," she assured him. "*We* are fine."

A flutter beneath his hand startled Tyler. He pulled the ineffective blanket down until it lay bunched on Chrissi's legs and only the light hospital gown covered her to her thighs. With both hands he touched her sides and slid them both toward the convex rise where the child had been and his mind began to open to the fact before him. The baby bump was still present.

Chrissi was mesmerized by Tyler's reverent touch. When his gaze caught on hers again, there was a guarded hopefulness – as if he didn't quite believe the evidence before him. On a ragged breath, he asked once more, "The baby? She's …?"

Chrissi's hands joined Tyler's, holding him steady physically; buoying him up emotionally. She nodded. "Yes," she whispered. "She's just fine."

The desperation in Tyler's voice and expression cut through any final remaining questions Chrissi might have harbored. The questions of whether he could fully love her child, considering the whole situation. At last she thought she understood the reason for Tyler's despondency and quietly asked, "You thought ... you thought we'd lost her?"

Tyler had laid his head lightly against the bump, as if he could hear something through the layers of tissue and skin; as if he could connect somehow with the child and let it reassure him that she was, indeed, fine. Chrissi let the fingers of one hand play in the dark waves of Tyler's hair as he rested there, drawing renewed strength. He had shifted his hand on top of her other hand and together they came as near as they could to holding the child – tenderly, lovingly. And then they both felt the swirling, fluttering sensation again. It was the baby moving vigorously.

Leaping for joy, Chrissi thought. She vaguely recalled that there was a passage in the Bible that referred to someone's baby leaping for joy and thought to herself that she would need to look that up and read it when she had time.

Swamped with relief and thankfulness, Tyler began to move to a chair but Chris stopped him. "Stay with me," she asked in entreaty. "Lay with me?" And so they rested together, spooned with the hospital blanket between them; her head on his arm, his hand on her abdomen; and the peace of God wrapped around the three souls.

CHAPTER TWENTY

"You look like something the cat dragged in," Jeff observed hours later as his gaze slid over his son who was slumped in a vinyl-covered hospital chair beside Chrissi's bed. Tyler might have been irritated, except that the statement was most likely an honest one – seeing as how he felt like something the cat dragged in. That, and he readily recognized the love in his father's voice.

Before Tyler could respond, Jeff swiveled his attention to Chrissi. "How's my favorite daughter-to-be?" he asked with fondness coloring his voice.

In an impish response she grinned and said, "You'll have to come closer before I'll answer." He complied and was surprised when Chrissi raised her arms in an invitation for a hug. After a quick embrace, she confirmed that she and the baby were both perfectly fine and she expected to be released later the same day. Tyler's look was skeptical, but Jeff didn't pursue the subject that was obviously a source of debate.

"Your mother and I wanted lots of kids," Jeff spoke, clearly addressing Tyler, although his eyes traveled from one bright and festive floral bouquet to the next. "It never worked out, of course. She suffered so many false alarms and miscarriages, but she refused to quit trying."

Not knowing what to say, neither Tyler nor Chrissi spoke.

"And then Mrs. Holmes showed up with you." He smiled sadly at the memory. "She was frantic," Jeff explained in a quiet tone. "She didn't want to tell Harold that she'd had a daughter when she was young and single and living away from Miller's Bend; but she had to make sure you were loved and cared for. And she came to us. Mary Beth latched onto you like you were going to save her life – or she was going to save yours. And after that, there was no way around keeping you."

Tyler stepped close to his father, offering support with a gentle hand to the older man's shoulder. "We've been reading the story, Dad," he said. "It had been so incredibly hard for Mrs. Holmes to leave her daughter behind with the baby's father's family, but she'd felt she had no choice. I get that. But ... we haven't gotten far enough in the manuscript to know about the day she brought me to you," he said as he gestured to the pages that lay on the table near Chrissi's bed. "If she never had contact with her daughter, how did Mrs. ... Grandma ... end up with me?"

"The girl had been told from early in life that her mother had abandoned her, and she had grown to hate Mrs. Holmes," Jeff explained. "I'm sure it's all in there," he said as he indicated the book. "The night she showed up in Miller's Bend with you, she told your grandmother that she'd discovered the truth when she had found dozens of letters sent by Mrs. Holmes over the years. Her family had kept the letters from her, reinforcing their story that her mother hadn't loved her. But with her father dead, no husband and a new baby, her life was spiraling out of control."

He paused. Breathed deeply. And faced Tyler. "She told Mrs. Holmes that since she had bailed out on raising her and the cosmos was evening the score, or some such nonsense. She handed over the baby – you – and left."

"And Mrs. Holmes panicked," Tyler filled in with a harsh sound that was a bit like a laugh, but not. "Because her husband didn't know about any of it."

"And she thought she was too old to raise a baby," Jeff confirmed. "Once Mary Beth had you in her arms, there was just no way I could make myself strip you away from her. Mrs. Holmes persuaded an old friend of hers who was a lawyer to make up the documents. And it was done."

Chrissi chimed in, asking, "What about the woman? Ty's birth mother?"

After a lengthy pause Jeff finally replied with a clipped, "She died." The chief's voice was oddly cold as he answered, almost mournful but with a touch of disdain. He faced Tyler at last. "I'm afraid she had a hard life."

He cleared his throat and strangled a noise deep in his chest. "A' course, we lost Mary Beth before you even had a chance to really know her. I did the best I could with you and it worked out alright for quite a while."

"You did a great job -" Tyler began only to have Jeff dispute the thought.

"I made mistakes – had shortcomings," he explained. "I thought things were getting on alright, but then you went and painted Mrs. Holmes' garage with Matt and Riley."

"That turned out to be a really good thing," Tyler countered. "For all of us."

"Sure enough," the older man confirmed. "She'd lost Harold the winter before and had been holed up in that house. Withering away, she was." He smiled sadly as he recalled. "She called me in tears that day, saying that a bunch of hoodlums were destroying her garage. Imagine my surprise when I responded to the call and found my own son."

"When we agreed on your punishment, it seemed like a good opportunity for her to get to know you, and for you to have the influence of a fine woman in your life," he related. "But she still never wanted to tell you the truth. Something about the prospect frightened her, even after all those years; even after we'd lost Mary Beth and Harold." He was quiet for a while then, as if recalling memories that had been stifled for years. He remained unfocused and seemed regretful as his gaze shifted to the window without any purpose.

"That's so sad," Chrissi offered when no one else spoke.

Her quiet comment seemed to bring Jeff from his errant thoughts. "If it's possible to find him, I'll use my resources to try to locate the man ... your father," he offered in a harsh low tone, as if it pained him to say the words. "If that's what you want."

Tyler's response was immediate and emphatic. "I know full well where my father is," he declared with fresh tears brimming in his gray eyes. Clasping the man who had raised him in a bear hug and then releasing him again, he explained, "My father is the man who loved Mary Beth Schuster. He's the man who sat with me when I had chicken pox, made me do my homework and study my confirmation lesson; he carried me to the hospital when I broke my leg in the city park. He instilled in me an appreciation for my elders, respect for women and hope for the next generation. You taught me how to be a caring, loving man of faith, and I will teach my children the lessons I've learned from you."

The door pushed open, startling them. "Oh, sorry," Melanie half-whispered as she entered the room. Apologetically she added, "I thought Chrissi was probably alone." However, she didn't hesitate or offer to retreat. Instead she turned toward her daughter and immediately enveloped Chrissi in a tearful hug.

Ashley appeared instantly, dashing to Tyler and wrapping her arms briefly around him. "Thank you," she breathed. "You saved our lives." Matt hovered close behind his wife, and although he didn't comment, deep gratitude shown in his expression. Tyler recalled that his friend had said something similar while leading him to Chrissi's room hours earlier.

Denial surfaced as Tyler tried to process what they were telling him. "I didn't do anything," he protested. "It couldn't have been that serious." His gaze darted to his father's face, searching for confirmation, but the older man's look was a grave one.

"It was that serious, son," Jeff confirmed. "They meant to kill Ashley and Rori."

"Kill them?!" Tyler asked in dismay.

Before anyone responded, Chrissi broke into the conversation. "What?" she demanded with fear coloring her voice. "What happened? Is Rori okay?"

Ridiculously, the whole group swarmed the young woman to keep her from trying to climb out of the bed. "Rori is fine," they assured her repeatedly.

"Tell me what happened," Chrissi directed from the hospital bed. She could have been speaking to anyone, but her gaze had zeroed in on her future father-in-law, the police chief.

He was shaking his head, even as the words finished falling into the space between them. "Can't do it," he stated in response. "I can't discuss an ongoing investigation. Not even with family." He turned his focus on Matt and Ashley, as if he intended to admonish them further. Instead he announced that he needed to return to the office and delve into the paperwork from the preceding evening.

Before the door closed completely behind Jeff, Byron slipped into the room carrying a vase filled with roses. An element of jealousy pinched in Tyler's chest – he should have been the person who'd brought roses to Chrissi. Why hadn't he thought of that? Emotional and physical exhaustion were to blame, he supposed regretfully. Even as other flower arrangements had been delivered, he'd failed to take the hint.

As her father set the vase on the table near the bed, Chrissi extended her arms toward the man. "Thank you, Dad."

Accepting the hug, Byron explained, "It wasn't my doing. I just met the floral delivery lady in the lobby. She said she'd been to your room several times already, so I offered to bring it in with me."

Chrissi's dark, expressive eyes filled with curiosity as she glanced to Tyler, who shrugged helplessly. His cell phone buzzed in his pocket and he reached for it. They both knew he hadn't left her room; that he hadn't called to order any flowers. He pulled the phone out and glanced at the screen. A text from Rori. Chrissi reached for the card and pulled it free of the envelope.

Take credit for the flowers, the text read.

Chrissi's forehead creased with confusion as she handed the card to Tyler. In a stranger's handwriting – undoubtedly that of a flower shop employee – the message read, "I love you with everything I am and everything I ever hope to be."

"Truer words were never delivered by proxy," Tyler said with a smile. He dropped a hip onto the bed next to his betrothed, and extended the cell phone to Chrissi, who accepted it and read the words silently.

When she raised her eyes to meet his, her face shown with open devotion. Tyler's breath caught as he took in her expression. She no longer simply accepted, admired, and yes, loved, him. Suddenly there was more. He responded to the emotions he interpreted, and drew close to her lips, but he paused. A rich blush rose in her cheeks when he pulled back, remembering that her family flanked the hospital bed.

He turned his attention to the others in the room. "So what really did happen last night?"

"Vengeance is a nasty force," Ashley began with a quaver in her voice. Matt's arm tightened around her shoulders, as if he could help protect her from the events already past, and her gaze was drawn to his. Tyler sensed that his friend was back on solid footing with his wife. They'd been in disagreement since the night Chris had revealed her pregnancy, but had been working to regain their closeness.

Ashley tenderly swept her fingers across the darkening bruises on Matt's face before turning her attention back to Chrissi and Tyler. She explained that after taking hundreds of photos during the grand march and the prom, she had gone to the office to download the files onto the server. "Since Matt was working late at the studio, I figured I may as well go ahead with the photo editing," she said. "I was working, and I must have heard a noise or something, because I looked up ... and there she was ... Bobbie."

The color drained from Ashley's cheeks, leaving her looking younger and more vulnerable than Tyler remembered seeing her before. She pulled in a shaky breath before continuing, as Matt continued to support her. "She was holding a gun, and said she would see me dead for my crimes," Ashley related. "When I asked what I'd done, she claimed I'd stolen the Chronicle away from her. In her mind, she had been certain that Charlie and Catherine were planning to gift the business to her, and that I had insinuated myself into their good graces and swindled them out of their livelihood."

"It turns out that all the things that happened at the newspaper when Ashley first arrived in town were Bobbie's ploys to try to drive Ashley away," Matt interjected.

Ashley nodded and pulled slightly back from Matt's hold. "We were so wrong when we accused Neal of doing those things," she confirmed. A thoughtful look crossed her expression as she paused. "I think it was good for him to move on, but I still feel bad for accusing him."

"Bobbie?" Chrissi nudged. "What did she do?" she asked as her dark eyes darted between her brother's and sister-in-law's faces.

"I got close enough to her to try to get the gun away," Ashley said with a shrug before Matt cut in.

"That was crazy," he attested. "You could have been killed."

"Would have been killed," his wife countered in a bold voice. She lifted her chin in defiance as she continued, "I couldn't just wait around – I had to do something." She shifted her attention back to Chrissi and Tyler, as Matt's parents had already heard the story. "I had nearly overpowered Bobbie when Adam showed up with Rori."

"With Rori?" Chrissi questioned in horror. "You mean -"

"As a captive," Matt interjected.

"He'd … subdued … her," Ashley explained with pain in her voice. "She's okay now," she added, when Chrissi looked as if she would climb out of the bed and leave in search of her friend. "She's at home with her folks. No worse for the wear."

"Adam fired his gun and the bullet hit the old oak desk in the back office," Ashley recounted as her gaze strayed toward the window. It seemed as if she needed to distance herself from her family members in order to maintain her collection. Absently, she touched her arm, near the shoulder, and winced. "The wood splintered," she said. "Some caught my arm. Some hit Bobbie in the face – in her eye, too."

Ashley told the gathering how Adam had lost control, when he thought he'd hit his own mother with the bullet. He'd thrown Rori into the corner, near a built-in vault. She'd jammed her injured wrist, but had remained silent. Ashley had moved to assist her, abandoning her attempt to get the gun Bobbie had brandished earlier. "I was afraid that if I came up with the gun, Adam would shoot me or Rori," Ashley spoke tearfully. "I couldn't risk it after she was there, too. The odds weren't on my side."

Tyler broke into the conversation, questioning the reason Adam had taken Rori to the Chronicle.

"We don't know if they planned to meet there or if Bobbie had called him to come and help, and he already had Rori, so he just brought her along," Matt answered.

"I was trying to figure out something, anything, to get us out of there alive," Ashley picked up the story again. "They argued a lot, and Rori and I prayed. And waited."

"How did you get all beat up?" Tyler asked Matt. "How did you know to go to Ashley's office?"

"I'd been at the studio until late, and Ash had let me know she was staying at the newspaper to work on the photos," he began. Matt picked up his wife's hand and pulled her close. "When I got home and she wasn't there, I went to the office to check on her."

"Totally unprepared," she added with a frail smile toward Matt.

"Totally," he agreed. Looking to Tyler and Chrissi, he elaborated, "I walked in the front door and strolled through the building humming, so they knew I was coming long before I stepped into the back office."

"Adam punched him," Ashley interrupted. "They knocked him unconscious and bound his wrists," she added indignantly. "Apparently, he looked tougher than I did," she huffed. "They didn't tie me up."

"You didn't fight back," Matt observed. "You weren't a threat."

"You weren't either!" she exclaimed. "You were knocked out."

"I woke up," he added dryly.

Tenderness pooled in Ashley's blue eyes as she touched a knob that was hidden in Matt's hair. "I'm really glad you did," she breathed. "Thank God."

"After that, they tied all our hands and locked us in the vault," Ashley said, bringing the conversation back on track. "Matt was struggling to get us all free, but we couldn't get the bindings off." She paused again, thinking of how near they had come to death.

When she didn't continue, Matt pressed on, revealing, "They were going to burn the building down, with us locked inside."

"That's when your dad showed up with his men," Ashley said to Tyler. "It was a miracle!"

"I've never been so glad to see Chief Schuster," Matt offered. "Some officers pulled us from the vault and he had

Brewer face down on the floor, a knee in his back and was cranking on the handcuffs."

"Rori's truly alright?" Chrissi asked. "He hadn't …" She turned scared eyes toward Tyler, but didn't ask outright.

He nodded, understanding her concern. "I will take you to see her before I take you home," he offered. "That way you'll be able to see for yourself how she is. Will that work?"

Matt and Ashley tried to assure everyone that Rori had not suffered from the incident. "I'm pretty sure she got beaten up worse the other time he tried to take her, when the Fields boy helped her," Ashley asserted.

"I thought Brewer was still in jail for that," Tyler challenged. Ashley explained that his mother, Bobbie, had bailed him out of jail. And the two had set out, whether independently or in tangent, to extract their own form of justice: Adam against Rori, the only person whose testimony would convict him; Bobbie against Ashley, who had "stolen the newspaper" from her.

The conversation wore down, and after the visitors left, Tyler spoke quietly to Chrissi. "I'm going to find Dr. Stapp," he informed her. When she might have protested, he explained, "I want to see if I can get you out of here." Sweetly, his lips brushed hers, and then he added, "You're not going to rest until you see Rori face to face, so I'd better get the wheels rolling."

Cadee Brystal

CHAPTER TWENTY-ONE

Chrissi leaned silently against the door jamb with a fuzzy, warm robe pulled tightly around her torso. The floorboards chilled her bare feet, but she didn't mind as she gazed upon her family rocking gently in the chair in the nursery. Her life, although it had seemed poised to spin wildly out of control just under a year ago, was good. It was sweet and full and she was submerged in happiness.

Bathed in the soft glow of green and red light cast by the outdoor Christmas lights, the man whom she loved clutched their baby girl in his powerful but loving arms as he gently rocked. The little girl had come into the world on Labor Day, which naturally made headlines in the local newspaper. She and Tyler had compiled a lengthy list of names prior to her birth, but as they'd held the child entrusted to them by God, they'd known that none of those names belonged to her. It had come to them the day after her birth that the precious little girl's name was Jessica, which Chrissi had discovered means "God beholds."

From the time of the wedding in June, Mrs. Holmes had referred unerringly to the unborn child as Joy. And although they had teased Tyler's grandmother, that she could be scarring a little boy for life, she'd been adamant that her moniker for the

243

child would do no harm. Once Chrissi and Tyler had agreed on Jessica as the first name, Joy became her middle name, almost without consideration.

As she looked upon the nursery room scene, the lyrics of the hymn "Amazing Grace" sounded in Chrissi's subconscious self, "The Lord has promised good to me, His Word my hope secures; He will my Shield and Portion be, As long as life endures."

Tears of happiness and gratitude welled in Chrissi's eyes. The Lord had promised good to His children, and although she knew the verse in the hymn relates to eternal life, she was eager to acknowledge that goodness was plentiful in her life on Earth as well. A verse from the Psalms sprang to mind and she thankfully recited it under her breath, "Hear, O Lord, and be merciful to me; O Lord, be my help. You turned my wailing into dancing; you removed my sackcloth and clothed me with joy, that my heart may sing to you and not be silent. O Lord my God, I will give you thanks forever."

Hearing her whispered prayer, Tyler looked up to find his wife watching from the doorway. His wife. Sometimes he could barely believe how lucky he was to have her in his life. The magnitude of his feelings swept through him and he cradled Jessica closer to his chest. With deep contentment, a slight sigh escaped from the child as she slept. They were lucky to have arrived at this place in their lives together and Tyler's heart echoed the words Chrissi had whispered.

They could have easily lost the precious child the night of the accident in May, and Chrissi had encountered some trouble during the delivery, but God had seen them through, protecting them and moving the fledgling family forward. But there was more. The love and support of their families had helped the couple bond together. And even though Tyler had been resistant to Rori's idea that the pair needed counseling, he'd gone.

The sessions with Dr. Kingston had helped Chrissi immensely, and for that Tyler was grateful, but he had grudgingly discovered that the counseling had been beneficial to him as well. Together they learned about family dynamics and how to relate to each other. Neither had grown up in a traditional home, and both gained relationship-saving insight as they grew as a couple.

Tyler's gaze was drawn back to Chrissi's form which was silhouetted in the doorway, back lit with light from the hall. He realized then that he hated the fuzzy robe – more specifically, he hated that she was wearing it. "You're coming back to bed, right?" she whispered.

He rose from the rocker and stepped so near to her that he could lightly cover her frigid toes with his own. Her light perfume tickled his senses as, still cradling Jessica in the crook of his left arm, he touched Chrissi's cheek tenderly with his right hand. She leaned toward him and delicately kissed Tyler's lips, before dropping her attention to the infant. "Sleep tight, sweetie," she whispered as her lips skimmed Jessica's forehead. And then peeking up through her eyelashes, the woman spoke to her man in a quiet tone, "Don't be too long."

After settling Jessica into the waiting crib, Tyler hurried back toward the room Chrissi had retreated to, and slipped between the covers. Rolling onto his side, he reached for her and she quickly snuggled against his solid body. His fingertips skimmed her thigh and then rested on the rise of her hip.

Her voice was already beginning to sound sleepy when she spoke, "I love you."

"And I love you."

A moment later, she sighed, "Ty?"

"Hmm."

"Was it a mistake?" she pondered as a yawn escaped.

Months ago, the comment might have caused an eruption of panic through his mind, racing to the dark corners of his consciousness, spreading light on his secret fears. But he'd grown in confidence in their relationship, and he knew their choice to marry had been the right decision.

"No. It wasn't a mistake," he said, hoping to build her confidence, even as he wondered what had caused her to reconsider.

"Oh." She sounded sad, as if she'd hoped he felt it was a mistake. "I just miss Miller's Bend … our friends … our families. I thought maybe we should move back."

Tyler's muscles tightened as he digested this comment. *Move back?* They had both given up their apartments in Miller's Bend, said their goodbyes and moved to Sioux Falls so Chrissi could attend the college she'd chosen. She only had one semester of classes completed, so how could they move back?

Cautiously he ventured, "How long have you been considering this idea?" She shifted, turning toward him, as if she could see his face and gauge his reaction.

"For a while ..." Her voice was so soft, as though she were afraid he'd be upset. He didn't speak, but waited, knowing she would reveal more of her thoughts if he gave her time. "It just hasn't felt right – being in the city. It doesn't feel like home." A shuddering sigh escaped from her before she said, "I'd been thinking we should see it through, stay the course, and all that. But tonight your grandmother's offer to give us this house if we want to return, just seems like the final confirmation that this is where we belong," she concluded.

Tyler's hopes opened up, maybe they could come back sooner than they had originally planned. He'd hired Mason's sister, Katie, as a manager for the nursery, and while she was a good worker, she had not turned out to be a good fit for a management position. Some personal issues had arisen in her life, and she'd quit. When Katie left Miller's Bend, it left Tyler with a huge problem in his business. He hadn't wanted to tell Chrissi that he was having trouble finding a new manager for the coming season.

But, his conscience pointed out, they'd decided together to live in Sioux Falls until Chrissi completed her education, and they had agreed to wait and decide what to do after that. "What about school?" he whispered gruffly. "You can't give up on your dreams."

Delicate fingertips touched his cheek, her thumb testing his lips a second before she kissed him. And then she responded, "Haven't I told you before? Dreams change."

He captured her hand, enveloping it in the rough warmth of his own, and inhaled deeply. He wanted too much to agree to the idea whispered in the dark – to return to his hometown – but something cautioned him against accepting it too quickly. "Let's sleep on it. We don't have to make a hasty decision. And I think we need to pray about it, too."

"But your grandmother ..."

"She'll understand," he replied with amenable patience. "She'll support us, no matter what we decide. And I doubt she would be critical of us taking it to the Lord. Everything will come in its own time."